THE APPLEBY FILE

Also by Michael Innes

THE APPLEBY FILE

DETECTIVE STORIES

MICHAEL INNES

DODD, MEAD & COMPANY · NEW YORK

First published in the United States 1976

Printed in the United States of America
by The Haddon Craftsmen, Inc., Scranton, Penna.

Library of Congress Cataloging in Publication Data

Stewart, John Innes MacKintosh, date.
    The Appleby file.

      CONTENTS: The Appleby file: The Ascham. Poltergeist.
The fishermen. The conversation piece. Death by water.
[etc.]
      1. Detective and mystery stories, English.
I. Title.
PZ3.S85166Aoe3   [PR6037.T466]   823'.0872   75-22398
ISBN 0-396-07279-8

CONTENTS

The Appleby File

Appleby's Holidays

THE APPLEBY FILE

THE ASCHAM

'I WON'T SWEAR,' Appleby said, 'that we haven't been mildly rash. But we'll get through.' He changed gear cautiously. '*With luck*, we'll get through. . . . Damn!'

The exclamation was fair enough. The car had been doing splendidly. At times, indeed, it seemed to float on the snow rather than cut through it, and when this happened it showed itself disconcertingly susceptible to the polar attractions—polar in every sense—of the bank rising steeply on its left and the almost obliterated ditch on its right. And now Appleby, steering an uncertain course round a bend, had been obliged to pull up—and to pull up more abruptly than was altogether safe. There was a stationary car straight in front, blocking the narrow road.

'Bother!' Lady Appleby said. 'It's stuck. We'll have to help to dig it out.'

Appleby peered through the windscreen. Snow was still lightly falling through the gathering dusk.

'It won't be a question of helping,' he said. 'If you ask me, it's abandoned. I'll investigate.' He climbed out of the car, and found himself at once up to the knees in snow. 'We've been pretty crazy,' he said, and plunged towards the other car.

Judith Appleby waited for a minute. Then, growing impatient, she climbed out too. She found her husband gazing in some perplexity at the stranded vehicle. It was an ancient but powerful-looking saloon.

'Abandoned, all right,' Appleby said, and tried one of the doors. 'Locked, too. Not helpful, that.'

'What do you mean, not helpful?'

'If we could get in, we could let the brake off, and perhaps be able to shove it aside. It's not all that snowed up, is it?'

'Definitely not.' Judith peered at the wheels. 'Engine failure, perhaps. But it stymies us.'

'Exactly. The driver got away while the going was good. Rather a faint-hearted bolt. And some time ago. There are footprints going on down the road. They've a good deal of fresh snow in them.'

'I suppose that must be called a professional observation. Let's get back into the car. I'm cold. But why didn't the silly ass stay put? It's the safest thing to do. And one can be perfectly snug in a stranded car.' She had kicked some of the snow from her feet and climbed back into her seat. She closed the door beside her. 'It's beautifully warm. Stupid of him to stagger off into the night.'

'Yes, wasn't it?' Appleby climbed in beside his wife. Their car was rather far from being a conveyance of the most modest order; the abandoned car was markedly humbler and less commodious. Appleby refrained from pointing this out. 'I do find it a shade puzzling,' he said. 'But our own course is fairly simple. We'll reverse as far as those last cross-roads. It can't be more than a mile. . . . Good Lord, what's that?'

'I rather think—' Turning in her seat, Judith looked through the rear window. 'Yes. It's something sublimely simple, John dear. An avalanche.'

Appleby looked too. 'Avalanche' was perhaps rather a grand word for what had happened. But there could be no doubt about the fact. The bank behind them was extremely steep; nevertheless a surprising depth of snow had contrived to gather on it; and this had now precipitated itself upon the road. Appleby had to waste little time estimating the dimensions of the resulting problem. Their car was trapped.

'Never mind, darling.' Judith, when cross, usually adopted a philosophical tone. 'There's some chocolate in the glove-box. And we can keep the engine running and the heater on. It's a good thing you filled up.'

'A good thing *I* filled up? You said—' Appleby broke off, having glanced at the petrol gauge. It was not one of those occasions upon which expostulation serves any useful purpose. 'There's under a gallon,' he said. 'And we haven't got a spare tin. Civilisation is always lulling one into a false sense of security.'

'But, surely, that's all right? Just ticking over, the petrol will last, won't it, for hours and hours?'

'Undoubtedly. Into the small hours, in fact.'

'The small hours?'

'Two in the morning. Perhaps three.'

'I see.' Judith, who had been contentedly breaking up a slab of chocolate, seemed a little to lose heart. 'John, when the heater stops, how long will the car take to . . . to get rather cold?'

'Oh, a quite surprisingly long time. Fifteen minutes. Perhaps even twenty.' Appleby picked up a piece of chocolate. 'I think,' he said rather grimly, 'you'd better get out the map. And I'll turn on this inside light. It's getting dark.'

'We *are* a surprisingly long way from the high road,' Judith said presently. 'I'd no idea.'

'Um,' Appleby said.

'There's that last sign-post. At least I think it is.'

'It's a reasonable conjecture.'

'I'd forgotten it was so deserted a countryside. There doesn't seem to be a hamlet, or a house, for miles. But wait a minute.' Judith's finger moved across the map. 'Here's something. "Gore Castle". Only it's in a funny sort of print.'

'That means it's a ruin. They use a Gothic type for places of archaeological or antiquarian interest.'

'But I don't think Gore Castle *is* a ruin—or not all of it.

I'm sure I've heard about it.' Judith seemed for the moment to have forgotten their depressed situation. 'Get out the *Historic Houses*.' Appleby did as he was told. The work was very much Judith's vade-mecum, and she flicked through its pages expertly. 'Here we are,' she said. 'Yes, I was quite right. Listen. "Three miles south of Gore. Residence of J. L. Darien-Gore Esqre. Dates partly from 13th century. Pictures, tapestry, furniture, stained glass, long gallery—" '

'I never heard of a mediaeval castle with a long gallery.'

'It must be the kind of castle that turns into a Jacobean mansion at the back. But let me go on. "—long gallery, formal gardens, famous well." '

'Famous what?'

'Well. A wishing-well, perhaps, or something like that. "April 1 to October 15—Thursdays only, 2–6. Admission 15p. Tea and biscuits at Castle. Catering facilities at Gore Arms, Gore." I knew I was right.'

'About the biscuits?'

'About its being inhabited. This Darien-Gore person—and I'm sure I've heard the name—'

'It does seem to recall something.'

'Well, he certainly lives there. We've only got to find the place and introduce ourselves.'

'I'd say we only have to find the place. No need to put on a social turn. The chap can't very well thrust us back into the night. Not that the question is other than academic. We can't possibly set out to find Gore Castle. It's almost dark already, and we'd be off the road in no time. That mightn't be a joke. The drifts must be pretty formidable.'

'But, John, I can see the castle. It's positively beckoning to us.'

'*See* it? You're imagining things. Visibility's presently going to be nil.'

'Over there to the right. Let your eye travel past the back of the stranded car. You see?'

'Yes—I see. But—'

'J. L. Darien-Gore Esqre has turned on a light—perhaps high in the keep, or something. It's rather romantic.'

'If it's high in the keep, it may be anything up to five miles away.'

'We can follow it for five miles.'

'My dear Judith, have some sense. Darien-Gore—if it is he —may turn the thing off again at any moment. We're able to see it at all only because it has stopped snowing—'

'Which is encouraging in itself.'

Appleby had produced a small pair of binoculars, and was focusing them on the light.

'I think it possibly is the castle,' he said, and slipped the binoculars back into his coat-pocket. 'But we mightn't have gone a hundred yards before we lost it for good owing to some configuration in the terrain.'

'Bother the terrain. And I'd say we can each carry a suitcase.'

'Dash it all!' Very incautiously, Appleby allowed himself to be diverted by this manoeuvre. 'We can't turn up on the fellow's doorstep as if he ran a blessed hotel.'

'I think it would be only considerate. Otherwise Mr Darien-Gore would have to send grooms and people to rescue our possessions.'

'Sometimes I think you are beginning to suffer from delusions of grandeur.' But Appleby was fishing the suitcases from the back of the car. He'd taken another careful look at that light, and decided it couldn't be very far away. The venture was worth risking. 'At least we've got a torch,' he said. 'So come on.'

They plunged into the snow. But Appleby paused again by the abandoned car. If the fellow had just contrived to steer into the side of the road, they themselves would probably have managed to get past the obstruction, and so be on their way by now. Appleby felt the radiator. He looked again at the surface of the road immediately in front. The snow was thick enough. But it wasn't as thick as all that. He shook his head, and trudged on.

II

'Not at all,' Mr Darien-Gore said. 'The gain is all mine—and my guests'. Most delighted to have you here.'

Jasper Darien-Gore was in early middle-age. Spare and upright, he would have suggested chiefly an athlete who has carefully kept his form—if he hadn't more obviously and immediately impressed himself as the product of centuries of breeding. His appearance was as thoroughly Anglo-Norman as was that of his castle. And he had the air of courteous informality and perfect diffidence—Appleby thought—that masks the arrogance of his kind.

'And I do hope,' Darien-Gore added, 'that this will prove a reasonably comfortable room.'

Appleby looked around him in decent appreciation. It was at least a rather more than reasonably splendid room. If it was comfortable as well—which seemed very likely—this hadn't been secured at the expense of disturbing the general mediaeval effect. The walls were hung with tapestries in which sundry allegorical events dimly transacted themselves; logs crackled in a fireplace in which it would have been possible to park a small car; there was an enormous four-poster bed. It was no doubt one of the apartments one could view (on Thursdays only) for half-a-crown. Appleby wasn't without an awkward feeling that he ought to produce a couple of half-crowns now.

'Ah!' Darien-Gore said. 'Here is my brother Robert. He has heard of the accession to our company, and has come to add his welcome to mine.'

It seemed to Appleby that these last words had been uttered less by way of politeness than of instruction. Robert Darien-Gore was not looking very adequately welcoming. He was much younger than Jasper, equally handsome, equally athletic in suggestion, and decidedly colder and more reserved. Heredity, perhaps, had dealt less kindly with him. His, in fact, was a curiously haunted face—and not the less so from its air of now quickly assuming an appropriate social mask.

'Robert,' Jasper said, 'let me introduce you to—' He broke off. 'By the way, I think it is *Lady* Appleby? But of course. I was sure I recognised your husband. One never knows whether it is quite civil to tell people one has spotted them from photographs in the public prints. Robert—Sir John and Lady Appleby. Sir John is Commissioner of Metropolitan Police.'

'How do you do. I'm so glad you found your way to Gore. It might have been awkward for you, otherwise.' Robert was producing adequate interest. It couldn't have been put higher than that.

'We couldn't possibly have been luckier,' Judith said. 'We had a guide-book, you know. And it said "Tea and biscuits at Castle". I had a wonderful feeling that we were saved.'

'And so you are, Lady Appleby.' Jasper Darien-Gore, who appeared to be more amused than his brother, nodded cordially. 'The kettle, I assure you, is just on the boil.'

Judith, Appleby thought, was made to take this sort of situation in her stride. One couldn't even say that she was putting on a social turn. She was just being natural. Judith, in fact, ought to have married not a policeman but an ambassador.

'I hope that being held up for a night isn't desperately inconvenient,' Robert said. 'And I really came in to ask at once whether we could do anything about a message. The snow has brought our telephone line down, unfortunately—and it's the same, it seems, at the home farm. But I think we might manage to get one of the men through to the village.'

'Thank you,' Appleby said. 'But there's no need for anything of the sort. Nobody's going to miss us tonight, and I'm sure we can get ourselves dug out in the morning.'

'Then, for the moment, I'll leave you.' Robert turned to his brother. 'They're amusing themselves in the gallery again. I'll just go and see they do nothing lethal.' With the ghost of a smile, he left the room.

'*Thank* you!' Judith was saying—not to her host, but to her host's butler, whose name appeared to be Frape. The fact that Frape himself had brought up their suitcases was a simple index of the grip Judith was getting on the place. '*There*, please.' Judith had pointed to an enormous expanse of oak—it might have been a refectory table of an antiquity not commonly come by—upon which the suitcases would modestly repose. She turned to Darien-Gore. 'It's so stout of you,' she said. 'Sheer pests hammer at your door, frost-bitten and *famished*'—Judith quite shamelessly emphasised this word—'and you don't bat an eyelid.'

'I had no impulse to bat.' Darien-Gore was amused. 'And, of course, one mustn't—not on one's own doorstep. But, come to think of it, I almost did—bat, I mean—shortly before you came. You see, somebody else has turned up : a fellow who had to abandon a car—'

'The car that prevented ours from getting through, I expect,' Appleby said.

'That may well be. And a perfectly decent fellow, I imagine. Yet I had an obscure impulse to get rid of him—or at least to murmur that Frape would fix him up comfortably—'

'I should be very willing to, sir.' Frape, who had been giving a little ritual attention to the appointments of the room, interrupted his employer. 'And it's not, I think, too late. Nothing very definite has been proposed.'

'Thank you, Frape—but I think not.' Darien-Gore had spoken a shade sharply, and now he waited until the butler had withdrawn. 'Frape finds the fellow not quite qualified to sit on the dais, as one might say. No doubt he's right. But of course he'll dine with us. Under the circumstances, any-thing else wouldn't be the hospitable thing. Perhaps I was put off when he told me his name was Jolly. Difficult name to live up to—particularly, of course, when your car has been stranded in the snow.'

'I wasn't terribly clear that his car *was* stranded,' Appleby said. 'He didn't say anything to suggest it had broken down?'

'I don't recall that he did. Oh, by the way.' Darien-Gore, who had appeared to be about to take his leave, now changed his mind, and walked over to a heavily curtained window. 'I'm terribly sorry that, in the morning, you won't find much of a view. This room simply looks out on the inner bailey —an enclosed courtyard, that's to say. Perhaps you can see it now. The sky's cleared a little, and there's a moon.' He drew back the curtain. 'Step into the embrasure, and we'll draw these things to again. No need to turn out the lights.'

Appleby and Judith did as they were told. The effect was suddenly to enclose them in a small darkened room, one side of which was almost entirely glass. And as a moon had certainly appeared, they were looking out on a nocturnal scene very adequately illuminated for purposes of picturesque effect. Directly in front of them, the keep of the castle was silhouetted as a dark mass—partly against the sky and partly against the surrounding snows. It was a bleakly rectangular structure at present encased in a criss-cross of metal and wooden scaffolding. This added to its grim appearance. It was like a prison that had been thrust inside a cage.

'You seem to have quite a job of work on hand, over there,' Appleby said.

'Perfectly true. The weather has halted it for a time, but during the autumn we had masons all over the Castle. The Office of Works pays for most of it, I'm thankful to say.' Darien-Gore laughed whimsically. 'Odd, isn't it? My ancestors built the place to defy the Crown, more or less. And now the Crown comes along, tells me I'm an Ancient Monument, and spends pots of money propping up my ruins.'

'Is that the famous well?' Judith asked. She pointed

downwards. The inner bailey was a virgin rectangle of un-trodden snow—part in shadow and part glittering in the moonlight. In the centre of it a low circular wall, about the size of a large cart-wheel, surrounded a patch of impene-trable darkness.

'Yes, that's the well. I see you must really have been read-ing that guide-book, Lady Appleby. It's certainly what everybody wants to see. We put a grid over it when the castle's being shown—otherwise we might have a nasty bill for damages one day.'

'But why is it famous?' Judith asked. 'Is there some legend connected with it?'

'Nothing of that kind. What's out-of-the-way about it is matter of sober fact. It oughtn't really to be called a well. Think of it as a shaft—an uncommonly deep one—going down to a subterranean river, and you get the idea of it. The guide recites Kubla Khan to them, you know. To the tourists, I mean.'

'How very strange!' Judith said. 'Where Alph the sacred river ran?'

'Exactly. And through caverns measureless to man. There's some vast underground system there in the limestone. Ever been to those caves outside Rheims, where you walk for miles between bottles of champagne? It's said to be like that here —only on a vastly larger scale. And, of course, no champagne.'

'Can it be explored?' Judith asked. 'By the kind of people who go pot-holing—that sort of thing?'

'Not possible, it seems. Cast anything down my well, and it's gone for ever. And that doesn't apply merely to orange-peel and threepenny-bits. If you wanted to get rid of an elephant, and no questions asked or askable, the well would be just the place. It's had its grim enough uses in the past, as you can guess.' Rather abruptly, yet with a touch of achieved showmanship, Darien-Gore closed the curtains. 'We

dine at eight,' he said. 'Before that, people often gather for
an hour or so in the gallery. At this time of year, it serves its
original purpose very well. All sorts of games are possible,
and we even manage a little archery. I don't know whether
either of you happens to be interested in that sort of thing.'

'I've tried archery from time to time,' Judith said. 'And
I'd like to improve.'

'Then you must have a go under Robert's instruction. He's
quite keen, I'm glad to say.' Darien-Gore paused, as if uncertain whether to proceed. 'As my small house-party consists
of intimates, perhaps you will forgive me if I say something
more about my brother. He is moody at times. In fact his
nervous health has not been good over the past year, and
allowances must sometimes be made for him. I think you
will like his wife, Prunella. She's a courageous woman.'

'And who else is staying at the Castle?' Judith asked.
She had received with the appropriate mild concern the
confidence just imparted to her.

'Well, there's Mr Jolly, whom you've heard about. By the
way, we've put him in the room next to yours. My glimpse
of him doesn't suggest that he will be quite as entertaining
as he sounds. Then there's my very old friend Ned Strickland
and his wife Molly—'

'How nice!' Judith said. 'We know them quite well.'

'That's capital—and shows, my dear Lady Appleby, how
well house-parties arrange themselves at Gore. The only
other guest is a fellow called Charles Trevor, who does
something or other in the City. We were at school together,
and have been trying out a revived acquaintance. And now
I'll leave you. The bells do ring, by the way—and just at
present there even appear to be young women who answer
them. But I don't know what my father would have thought
of running Gore on a gaggle of housemaids.'

'A gaggle of housemaids.' Appleby was opening his suitcase
with an expression of some gloom. 'I suppose one might call

19

that rather a territorial joke. Would you say I'd better put on this damned dinner-jacket?'

'Yes, of course. And it's lucky I brought a decent frock.'

'Our fellow waif-and-stray, Mr Jolly, won't have a dinner-jacket.'

'You'll find that one or another of the Darien-Gores will keep him company by not dressing. But the other men will.'

'Oh, very well.' Appleby had little doubt that it would turn out just as Judith said.

'We're lucky to have hit upon such civilised people. And I look forward to seeing the Stricklands.'

'My dear Judith, General Strickland is an amiable bore.'

'Yes—but he's a very old friend of the family. Get him in a corner, and he'll tell you all about the Darien-Gores. I'm curious about them.'

'I'm sure you are. But I doubt whether there's a great deal to learn. I've a notion that Jasper was once a distinguished athlete—'

'Yes, that rings a bell. Something aquatic—high diving or water-polo or—'

'No doubt. And he's simply lived on his rents ever since. As for the melancholic Robert, perhaps the less one learns the better.'

'Just what do you mean by that?' Having found the dress she wanted, Judith was shaking it out on its hanger. 'You don't think he's mad, do you?'

'I'd hardly suppose so. But when a chap like Jasper Darien-Gore starts apologising for his brother in advance, one has to suppose there's something rather far wrong. And I've an impression that Robert, and presumably his wife Prunella, aren't simply here on a week-end visit. In some obscure way, Robert has taken refuge here. And you and I, my dear, butting in in the way we have butted in, have very precisely the social duty to discover nothing about it.'

'Perhaps we have. Only it's not in your nature, John, to refrain from looking into things—just as you're doing now.'

This was fair enough. Turning out his pockets as he changed, Appleby had come upon the binoculars he had first used in search of Gore Castle. He had drawn back a curtain and was using them now to take a closer look at the inner bailey. The moon was rising, and the sky had blown clear. Straight opposite, the keep was no longer a mere dark mass within its scaffolding. One could make out something of the detail of its surface, pierced by narrow unglazed windows. Below, the carpet of snow, untrodden even by the tracks of cat or bird, surrounded the sinister well.

'Come along,' Judith said. 'We mustn't skulk.'

Appleby closed the curtain and put down the binoculars. They left the room together. A few paces down the corridor, there was a half-open door on their right. And it was true that Appleby could seldom refrain from looking into things. He did so now. A middle-aged man, sharp-featured and indefinably furtive, appeared to have turned back into the room when about to leave it. He was now transferring from a small suitcase to a jacket pocket what appeared to be a rather bulky pocketbook.

'Well, well!' Appleby had walked on for some paces before he murmured this. 'Not only do we know the Stricklands. We know Mr Jolly as well.'

'Nonsense! I took a glance at the man. I'm certain I've never seen him before.'

'All right. But *I* know Mr Jolly quite well. Possibly he doesn't know me.'

'I don't see how—'

'I know him by sight, I ought to say. I've had the advantage of studying his photograph.'

'You mean he's a criminal?'

'He's thought to be. Perhaps it wouldn't be fair to put it stronger than that.'

'Then he's in for a fright when he discovers who you are.'

'I suppose he's bound to do that. Yes, I suppose Darien-Gore is bound to tell him.'

'Hadn't *you* better tell Darien-Gore—I mean, that he's sheltering somebody who may be after the family silver?'

'Perhaps so.' Appleby frowned. 'Only, it mightn't be altogether tactful. You see, Mr Jolly's line happens to be blackmail.'

'How revolting! But surely—'

'I think,' Appleby said, 'we go up this staircase to reach the famous long gallery.'

III

'One moment, my lady, if you please.' Frape had stepped forward rather dramatically out of shadow. 'You would find it safer to come up by the staircase at the other end of the gallery.'

'You mean that this one may tumble down?' Judith looked in some alarm behind her. It had been a stiff climb.

'Nothing of that kind, my lady. But to enter the gallery by this door—' Frape broke off as a sharp twang made itself heard from the direction in which he was pointing. 'That would be Mr Robert,' he said. 'Or it might be Mr Charles Trevor. Both draw a powerful bow. If that indeed be the correct expression among archers. . . . Ah!' The twang had made itself heard again.

'I think I see what you mean,' Appleby said. 'It wouldn't be healthy to get in the way of *that*.'

'Precisely, sir. But in a moment the round—if they call it that—will be over. You and her ladyship can then enter. Meanwhile, sir, may I ask if you have seen anything of Mr Jolly?'

'Yes—and I imagine he's coming along.'

'I am glad to hear it, sir. It had occurred to me that he might be lingering awkwardly in his room.' Frape turned to Judith. It was clear that he regarded her as worthier of the august confidence of an upper servant than was her husband.

'To my mind,' he murmured, 'an error of judgement on Mr Robert's part. Persons are best accommodated according to their evident station. Mr Jolly would have done very well in the servant's hall. And I could have answered for it that there would be no complaints.'

'I'm sure there wouldn't,' Judith said.

'Precisely, my lady. My own service has always been in large establishments and among the old gentry. In such circumstances one becomes accustomed to entertaining odd visitors from time to time. Even chauffeurs are occasionally odd. And lady's maids, I am sorry to say, are becoming increasingly so—as your ladyship is doubtless aware.'

'I haven't had one since I came out. So I wouldn't know.' Judith spoke with a briskness that doubtless characterised—Appleby thought—the old gentry rather than the new. But now, from beyond the door over which the communicative Frape stood guard, there came a small sound as of polite applause. 'They must have finished the end.'

'The end, my lady?'

'It's called an end, Mr Frape, not a round.'

Appleby, who would have addressed Frape as Frape, and who knew nothing about ends, felt that Judith had smartly scored two points at once.

'In other words,' he said, 'we can go in.'

'Exactly so, sir.' And Frape, with a grave bow, opened the door of the long gallery.

'As you'll notice, we manage fifty yards—which is quite a regular ladies' length. And there's plenty of height, as you see.' Prunella Darien-Gore was explaining this to Judith—and with a shade of desperation, Appleby thought. Her husband, who ought to have been giving these explanations, seemed to be sunk in a sombre reverie. 'Mr Trevor, will you show Lady Appleby?'

'Yes, of course.' Charles Trevor was stout and flabby; one would have guessed that he was without either interest or skill in athletic pursuits. But now he slipped on brace and tips, and with a casual certainty sent one arrow into the gold and two into the red. 'Robert?' he said challengingly.

Robert Darien-Gore came out of his abstraction with a start, and picked up his own bow without a word. Appleby, standing beside Robert's wife, was aware of a curious tension in her as she watched. He spoke out of an impulse in some way to relieve this.

'I know nothing about archery,' he said. 'But it's my guess that your husband is pretty good?'

'He used to be.' Prunella, Appleby saw, was digging her nails hard into the palms of her hands. 'It came second only to his rock-climbing.' She gave a suppressed gasp, as if suddenly aware that she was thinking of her husband as somebody out of the past. 'Yes,' she said. 'Robert is first-class. Watch.' Her sudden faith in her husband was justified. Robert shot three arrows and bettered Trevor's score. Into his final shot he appeared to have put unnecessary force. The shaft had buried itself deep in the heart of the target. In the middle ages, Appleby remembered, an arrow from an English long bow could pierce the thickest armour. And there was something alarming in this one. Its feathered tip was still quivering as he watched.

'Capital, my dear Robert!' General Strickland, who had been talking to Jasper Darien-Gore in a corner, set down a glass in order to applaud vigorously. 'Let's see if Trevor can beat that—eh? Just let me retrieve the things.' He turned to Appleby. 'We don't manage two ends, you see. It would lose us five yards we can't spare. So we shoot only from this end. Nobody do anything careless, please!' He hurried off down the length of the gallery.

'Ned isn't in Robert's class,' Mrs Strickland said to Judith. 'Nor in this Mr Trevor's either. But he can give Jasper a good match. I'm very much afraid he may want to now. Aren't you famished, Judith?'

'Quite famished. I suppose we're waiting for Mr Jolly.'

'Mr Jolly—whoever is he?'

'The other gate-crasher. He seems to have made the haven of Gore Castle about an hour before John and I did.'

'How very odd. I hope he isn't keen on archery too. I find it tedious—and a little unnerving.'

'Unnerving, Molly? I suppose it has a lethal background —or history. But—'

'I think it's that terrible twang—like something going wrong with a piano. But here they go again.'

General Strickland had retrieved the arrows, and now Charles Trevor was again addressing himself to the target. He sent his first arrow into the gold.

'There!' Mrs Strickland said. 'Didn't you hear? Like something happening to the poor old family Bechstein—or perhaps to one's grand-daughter's 'cello—in the middle of the night. Have you never been wakened up by just that?'

'I have.' Appleby, who had been accepting a drink from Frape, paused beside her. 'But, you know—'

'*Stop!*'

It was the vigilant Frape who had given this shout. And he was only just in time. As Trevor drew back the bow-string the door at the farther end of the gallery had opened, and Jolly had walked in. Not unnaturally, he stood trans-fixed, staring up the gallery at Trevor. And, for an alarming moment, Trevor himself oddly swayed, and with a queer and involuntary movement seemed almost to train his arrow upon the newcomer. Then he let his bow gently unflex. There was a moment or two of mild confusion, followed by intro-ductions. These last were not without awkwardness. Jolly seemed indisposed to make any claim upon the social graces. He gave each of the women in turn what was no doubt meant for a bow, but had more the appearance of a wary cringe. His glance tended to go apprehensively towards Trevor—as it still well might—and then travel furtively towards Robert. Frape stood in the background. It was evident that the proceedings were very far from enjoying his approval.

'Lady Appleby,' Jasper was saying. 'And Sir John Appleby. Sir John is—'

'How do you do?' Without too great an effect of abruptness, Appleby had cut explanations short. 'We're in the same boat, you and I. My car got stranded behind yours. Was it just the snow held you up, or did you have engine trouble?'

'A little bit of one thing and a little bit of another.' Jolly, whose address was no more polished than his manner, eyed Appleby narrowly. 'Acquainted with these people here, are you?' he asked.

'I happen to know General Strickland and his wife. But not the others.'

'I'm a stranger here myself. They invited me to stay the night. Affable, you might say. Not that they could well do anything else. Plenty of room in a place like this.'

'Clearly there is.'

'And no need to stint, either. Money in a big way, eh? And a touch of real class as well. I've a fancy for that. High aristocratic feeling. Sense of honour and so on.' Jolly gestured at the line of family portraits which hung in the long gallery. 'Eyes of one's ancestors upon one, eh? There's something I like about that.'

'No doubt you find it professionally advantageous. By the way, I gather you've met Mr Trevor before?'

'Trevor?' Jolly was startled. 'Who is he? Never heard of him.'

'He's the man who was about to shoot when you came into the gallery. I got the impression that you were looking at each other with some kind of recognition.'

'Nothing of the kind. What I recognised was that he very nearly killed me.'

'I don't know that he did quite that. But it was an awkward moment, certainly. It was natural that he should be agitated—that he should be a little agitated. I think I must go and have a word with him.'

'Does one require a licence,' Appleby asked casually, 'to play around with bows and arrows?'

'Good Lord, no!' Charles Trevor glanced at Appleby in surprise—and also, perhaps, with a faint impression of quick alarm. 'Why ever should one?'

'It has occurred to me that the things are just as efficient weapons as pistols and revolvers—more efficient than some. I've seeen that you can put an arrow through the pin-hole—isn't it called?—on that target. I doubt whether you could do the same thing with an automatic.'

'I've never handled a pistol in my life, so that's no doubt true.'

'Ah! Now, suppose that incident a few minutes ago had really resulted in an accident. Suppose you'd fired—or does one say shot?—dead at this fellow Jolly. You'd actually have transfixed him, wouldn't you?'

'Really, my dear sir! I don't know that it's very pleasant to—'

'He'd have been pinned to the wall, like a living butterfly that some cruel child—'

'Dash it all—' Not unreasonably, Trevor appeared outraged by this macabre before-dinner chat.

'I was only thinking, you know, that if one had sufficient cause really to hate a man, an arrow might be a more attractive weapon than a bullet. But you must forgive me. I'm a policeman, remember. My mind runs on these matters from time to time. And—do you know?—I can almost imagine that some people *would* hate Mr Jolly—quite a lot. I'd say he's a type one rather likes to forget about. Supposing when one *had* forgotten him—'

'I care nothing for this fellow Jolly. And I certainly don't think him worth talking about.'

'I was going to say that when the Jollys of this life *do* bob up again, the desirable thing is probably to keep one's head. As for talking—well, he's at least not a very conversable character himself. Look at him now.'

Jasper and General Strickland were competing against each other, though in rather a casual way. The others were engaged in desultory conversation behind them. Jolly, however, had retired to a window-seat at the side of the gallery. And he began, as Appleby looked, to fumble in a pocket. He might have been hunting for a cigarette-case or a box of matches. But what he brought out was a dark, bulky pocket-book. It was familiar to Appleby already. He had seen it, through the open bedroom door, going into Jolly's pocket earlier in the evening. Having produced it, Jolly did nothing more. He simply sat immobile, with the thing in his lap.

Appleby turned back to the others. He was just in time to catch a swift impression of the Darien-Gore brothers, momentarily immobile, gazing into each other's eyes. Then Jasper drew back his bow-string, and there followed the twang to which Molly Strickland took such exception. The shaft flew wide. There was a moment's silence in the gallery. It was broken by Frape.

'*Dinner is served*!'

IV

'I shall be delighted to have coffee in the gallery,' Mrs Strickland said as she re-entered it. 'I don't know a more charming room. But I make one condition—that those tiresome bows and arrows be put away. Judith, you agree?'

'I think I do. If the men find more talk with us boring, they can go away and play billiards.'

'Prunella, dear, you are hostess.' Mrs Strickland spoke a shade sharply. 'The onus is on you.'

'But of course!' Robert's wife had walked into the room in an abstraction. Now she turned round with a start. 'Only you needn't be anxious, Molly. There's never any archery after dinner. Jasper would as soon think to settle down to talk about money. Everything has been put in the ascham.'

'The what, dear?' The three women were alone, and Mrs Strickland was helping herself to coffee.

'Oh, I'm so sorry.' Prunella had again started out of inattention. 'The ascham is the name given to the cupboard where bows and things are kept. There it is.' She indicated a tall and beautiful piece of furniture, perhaps Elizabethan in period, which stood against the wall. 'I think it must be named after some famous archer.'

'Roger Ascham,' Judith said, a shade instructively. 'He wrote a book called *Toxophilus*. He was a schoolmaster.'

'I am sure he was an excessively dreary person.' Mrs Strickland was studying a row of bottles. 'Why, in bachelor establishments, are women of unblemished reputation invariably confronted with *Crème de Menthe*? Never mind. There's a perfectly respectable brandy too.'

'I am sure there is.' Prunella spoke rather drily. 'And won't you have a cigar?'

'Only at home, dear. That has always been my rule.'

Judith, too, found herself some brandy. So far, the evening had not been a success, and it appeared unlikely that it would perk up now. Dinner, indeed, had been so constrained an affair that the tactful thing would probably be an acknowledgement of the fact, made upon a whimsical note.

'John and I did our best,' she said. 'But we were foreign bodies, I suppose. It all *didn't* seem to mix terribly well.'

'One must blame that really *sombre* Mr Jolly,' Mrs Strickland said. 'He disappointed me. One so seldom has an opportunity of meeting that sort of person—unless one goes canvassing at election-time, or something of that kind. But he *quite* refused to be drawn out.'

'I'm afraid Robert was rather silent.' Prunella was gazing into her untasted cup of coffee. 'But he has been depressed ever since he . . . he resigned his commission. Jasper is very good—'

'One can see that they are devoted to each other,' Judith said.

'Yes—Jasper wants Robert to take over the running of the estate. I hope he will. It would be so much better than . . . than simply hanging around.'

There was an awkward silence, resolutely broken by Mrs Strickland.

'Jasper did his best with us—at dinner, I mean. He can talk so well about the history of Gore. Of course, I've heard parts of it before. But he told us some things that were quite new. About the ghost that walks in this gallery. I'm sure I never heard of that. Do you think it goes about pierced by an arrow? I wouldn't be at all surprised. And the superstition about the well at midnight—'

'There's a superstition about the well?' Judith asked.

'Yes. Didn't you hear? And I'm quite sure that *I* wouldn't care— But here are the men. I had a notion they wouldn't linger very long.'

'A very good dinner,' General Strickland said to Appleby. The two men were sitting in a corner of the gallery apart. 'A very good dinner, indeed.'

'It might have been a shade more lively, I thought.'

'Lively? I don't believe in dinners being lively. Not with a Margaux like that. Chatter spoils one's concentration, if you ask me.'

'Margaux, was it? Judith said it tasted rather like cowslip wine.'

'My dear boy, she was perfectly right. She always is. That's the precise description for the bouquet of Margaux. Ever been to the Château?' Strickland paused to sniff at his brandy. 'I must tell you, one day, of the week I spent there in '17. Absolutely amazing. Not that the place is anything much to look at. Not a patch on Gore. Built by some fellow called Lacolonilla about a hundred years ago, and might be

round the corner from my own house in Regent's Park. . . .
How does Gore strike you, by the way?'

'It's an impressive place—particularly to tumble into out
of the snow. And perhaps a shade oppressive, as well.'

'Never struck me that way. But then I've known it, you
see, man and boy. . . . Bit of a cloud over it at the moment,
eh?'

'So I feel. But Judith and I are unbidden guests, you
know. I told her, earlier this evening, that curiosity isn't on.'

'And she said that, with you, it's never off?'

'Well, as a matter of fact, she did.' Appleby paused to
light a cigar. 'But, Strickland—do you know?—I'm not sure
I wouldn't like any gossip there is. I've a notion there's
something . . . well, building up. Any idea what I mean?'

General Strickland looked about him cautiously. But the
two men were unobserved—except by the ancestral Darien-
Gore portraits on the walls.

'That fellow Charles Trevor seems deucedly uneasy,' he
said. 'And what's he doing here, anyway? Knows his spoons
and forks, and all that. In fact, he was at school with Jasper.
But not our sort. Not our sort, at all.'

'I suppose not.' Appleby was amused by this obscure social
judgement. 'But I imagine he's more our sort than poor
Mr Jolly.'

'Well, that's different. Very decent, unassuming chap, no
doubt. Some sort of counter-jumper or motor-salesman, eh?
Jasper didn't want to bother the servants with him.'

'So I've gathered—if it was Jasper. I rather think it may
have been Robert. There's a faint conflict of evidence on the
point.'

'Well, it comes to the same thing, my dear boy. The
brothers are tremendously thick. And, since Robert and
Prunella came to live here—'

'Why did they come?'

'Ah—that's telling.'

'I know.'

'Appleby, you really feel there's something ₂.. well, *happening* in this place?'

'Happening, or going to happen. Don't you?'

'That could be stopped?'

'Well, not by me. I just don't know enough.' Appleby paused to look into his brandy glass. 'Were you going to tell me about Robert?'

'My dear chap, *I* don't know. Nobody does—or wants to, I should hope. It looked damnably ugly for a time. And then it ended on what you might call a minor note.'

'Ended? What ended?'

'Robert's career, I suppose one has to say. He left the army. And the thing dropped.'

'The thing? What thing?'

'God knows, something there turned out not to be sufficient evidence about, I imagine.' General Strickland broke off, and again looked about him. This time, it was at the line of portraits silent on the wall. 'A poor show of some sort. Hard on a decent family, eh? Not much wrong with them since the Crusades, and all that.'

'You're a romantic at heart, Strickland. And *noblesse oblige* is all very well, no doubt.' Appleby was speaking seriously. 'But that particular sense of obligation is an open invitation to pride.'

'And pride?'

'Is an open invitation to the devil.'

'Here's Jasper coming down the gallery. He *looks* proud, I'm bound to admit. But he's ageing, too. It's just struck me. Still, he's kept his form. A great athlete, you know, as a young man. But not the sort that falls into a flabby middle-age. . . . I think he's coming over to talk to you. I must go and have another word with your wife. Astonishing thing, you two turning up here like that. Quite astonishing.'

'Delightful that you turned out to know the Stricklands,'

Jasper Darien-Gore said. 'Won't you and your wife treat it as an inducement to stay on for a day or two?'

'It's most hospitable of you, but I'm afraid we can't.' Appleby felt no reason to suppose that Darien-Gore had spoken other than merely by way of civility. There was, indeed, something faintly distraught in his manner which emphasised the point. 'As a matter of fact, we must try to get away fairly early.' Appleby hesitated, and then took a plunge. 'Unless, that is, I can be useful in any way.' He waited for a response, but none came. Darien-Gore was looking at him with a frozen and conventional smile. He simply mightn't have heard. Having begun, however, Appleby went on. 'You'll forgive me if I'm talking nonsense. But it has just occurred to me that in that fellow Jolly you may find yourself rather far from entertaining an angel unawares. And I happen to know—'

'Jolly?' Darien-Gore repeated the name quite vaguely. 'An odd chap, I agree. But he has been getting on quite well with Robert. In fact, they've been making some kind of wager—I've no idea about what.'

'I don't think I'd be inclined to lay any wager with Jolly. Winning and losing might prove equally expensive.'

'And he says that he must try to get away quite early, too. Ah, here he is.'

This was not wholly accurate. Jolly had been standing some little way across the gallery, and without showing any disposition to approach. But Jasper had made a gesture which constrained him to come forward.

'Mr Jolly,' he said, '—you must really leave us in the morning, if your car can be got away? It would be pleasant if you could stay a little longer.' As he produced this further civility, Jasper gave Appleby a hard smile. 'And, of course—' He broke off. 'Ah—thank you, Frape.'

Frape's appearance was with a large silver tray, upon which he was carrying round a whisky decanter, glasses, ice and a syphon. The Darien-Gores, it was to be supposed, kept

33

fairly early hours. Frape was looking particularly wooden. He had presumably overheard his employer's latest essay in hospitality.

'Very much obliged,' Jolly said. 'But fast and far will be my motto in the morning. All having gone well, that's to say.' He gave a laugh which was at once insolent and apprehensive. 'Yes, all having gone well.' He looked indecisively at the tray—and at this moment Robert Darien-Gore came up. Silently, he poured a stiff drink, added a splash of soda-water, and handed the glass to Jolly. Jolly, who already seemed slightly drunk, gulped, hesitated, gulped again. The two brothers watched him fixedly. He returned the glass, only half-emptied, to the tray, and waved Frape away. Frape's eyes met Appleby's for a moment, and then he moved silently off.

'I know just when I've been given enough,' Jolly said. 'And it has been the secret of my success.' He turned to Appleby, and gave him a look of startling contempt. 'Pleasant to meet people one has heard about,' he said. 'Isn't that right, Sir John?'

'Decidedly. And I'm glad, Mr Jolly, that I've been here to meet you tonight.'

'I know, you see, just how much I can take.' Jolly pointed at Appleby's glass, as if further to explain this remark. 'That, and fast and far, are the secrets of my success.'

'Come and have a final word with my wife, Mr Jolly.' Quite firmly, Appleby took Jolly by the elbow and led him away—leaving the Darien-Gores looking at each other silently. But Appleby took no more than a few paces towards Judith. 'My man,' he said, 'let me give you a word of advice. Stick, on this occasion, to fast and far. And make it quite clear that you have forgotten the other part of your secret of success.'

'I don't know what you're talking about.'

'I'm talking about life and death. Good night.'

V

'Good night, madam . . . good night, sir . . . good night, my lady.' Frape, standing at one of the doors of the long gallery, responded to such salutations as he was offered while the company dispersed. His employer and his employer's brother were the last to leave the gallery; to each of the Darien-Gores, as he very slightly bowed, he gave a grave, straight look. Jasper hesitated when at the head of the staircase, half-turned as if about to speak, thought better of it, and moved on. Robert had already vanished; in a moment Jasper's shoulders —squarely held—and then his head vanished too. Frape closed the door behind him, turned, and looked down the long gallery. From its far end the archery target regarded him like a staring and sleepless eye. He moved down the gallery, set glasses on a tray, placed a guard carefully before the great fireplace, turned off the lights, so that it was now by the flicker of firelight that he was lit, paused to look thoughtfully at the line of portraits on the wall. He went over to the ascham and saw that it was locked. He moved to a window, drew back a curtain, and stood immobile before the wintry scene. Small clouds were drifting across a high, full moon, so that pale light and near-blackness washed alternately over the landscape. To his left, and from very high up, he had an oblique view of the inner bailey; this came into full light for a moment, revealing the well still amid its unbroken carpet of snow.

Frape remained motionless, with the firelight flickering behind him.

V I

'Snubbed,' Appleby said.

'Never mind, darling. This is a most comfortable bed. And do hurry up. I'm extremely sleepy.' Judith put down

35

the book she had been reading. 'You mean you scrapped that business about having a social duty to discover nothing?'

'More or less.' Appleby took off his black tie and tossed it on the dressing-table. 'At least, I decided that I ought to offer our host some sort of warning about Jolly. What I was after was a little candour before trouble blows up.'

'What sort of trouble?'

'Unfortunately, I can't take more than a guess at it. If I could do more, it might be possible to act. Anyway, our friend Jasper refused to play. So did Jolly.'

'Jolly! You talked to him?'

'He's up to mischief, and I had a shot at scaring him off. It didn't work. You'd take him to be rather an apprehensive little rat, but in fact he has a nerve. It amuses him to be operating—and he certainly is operating—right under my nose.'

'He's gathered who you are?'

'Quite clearly he has. But I don't seem to carry around with me much of the terror of the law.'

'There's something between him and that man Charles Trevor.'

'I know there is.' Appleby was now in his pyjamas.

'I think Trevor is quite as nasty as Jolly. Perhaps they're confederates.'

'Perhaps.'

'You say something's going to happen. What?'

'Well, for one thing, you and I are going to sleep.' Appleby turned out a light. 'For another—but this is where I just start to guess—there's going to be some hard bargaining at Gore. And not of a kind, unfortunately, at which I can very well act as honest broker.'

'It sounds most unpleasant.'

'I'm sure it is. But I don't see there is anything I can do. I must think twice before compounding a felony, I suppose. And that's why, in a way, I don't really want to learn more. We didn't stagger in here out of the snow in order to start blowing police whistles and insisting on open scandal. Or that's how I see it at the moment. It may be different in the morning.' Appleby crossed to the window, drew back the curtain a little way, and half-opened a casement. He moved back across the room, got into bed, and turned out the last light. The room was quite dark, with only a narrow band of moonlight falling on a wall and across the bed. 'And now you're going straight to sleep,' he said.

The band of moonlight had moved a little; it now caught the corner of a picture. Otherwise the room was in absolute darkness. The only sound was Judith's breathing.

'*Twang*!'

Appleby found that he had come awake with a start, and that his mind was groping for the reason. And the reason came to him, like an echo on the inward ear, as he sat up and switched on a bedside lamp. Judith was still fast asleep.

He picked up his watch and looked at it; the time was just two o'clock. He slipped out of bed, went over to the door and listened intently. He came back, put on his dressing-gown, felt in his open suitcase and produced a pocket torch. Returning to the door, he opened it gently, went out, and closed it behind him. The corridor before him was quite dark and very cold. He let the beam from his torch first play down its empty length, and then circle until it found the door of Jolly's room. He went over to this, listened for some seconds, and then switched off the torch and cautiously turned the handle. The door swung back with a faint creak upon blackness. He switched on the torch again, and the beam fell on Jolly's shabby suitcase, open and untidy. The beam circled the room and fell upon the bed. It had been turned down at one corner. But nobody had slept in it.

Appleby closed the door—and as he did so heard faint sounds from the end of the corridor. They might have been slippered footfalls. He turned in time to see a dim form and a flickering light disappear round a corner. Muffling the torch in the skirt of his dressing-gown, he followed.

Under these conditions, Gore Castle seemed tortuous and enormous. Several times he lost all trace of the figure in front of him. And then, suddenly, he oriented himself. The newel by which he was standing belonged to one of the two stair-cases leading to the long gallery. He looked up. An unidentifiable male figure—like himself, in a dressing-gown, but holding a lighted candle before him—was disappearing into the long gallery itself. Appleby climbed rapidly. The gallery, when he reached it, was part in near-darkness and part floating in moonlight. At its far end stood the target, commanding the long, narrow place. Appleby rounded a screen, and the man with the candle stood before him. It was Frape. His hand was on the door of the ascham.

'What's this about, Frape?'

The candlestick in Frape's hand gave a jump. But when he turned round it was to look at Appleby steadily enough.

'The door of the ascham, sir. It seems to have been left unsecured, and to have been banging in the night. The fault is mine, sir. I am deeply sorry that you, too, should have been disturbed by it.'

'Nonsense.'

'I beg your pardon, sir?'

'You are talking nonsense, Frape, as you very well know.'

'I assure you, sir—'

'Open the door of the thing, and let's have a look. It's no more than you were going to do for yourself.'

Silently, Frape turned back and opened the door of the tall cupboard.

'Commendable,' Appleby said. 'Everything as accountable as in a well-ordered armoury. Those two empty places in the rack, Frape—I think they mean two arrows missing?'

'It might be so, sir. I cannot tell.'

'Two gone.' Appleby lifted a third arrow from the rack

and poised it in his hand. 'Simply as a dagger,' he said, 'it would make a pretty lethal weapon—would it not?'

'I really can't say, sir.'

'But there's a bow missing as well?'

'There may be, sir. I have never counted them, so am not in a position to say.'

'Frape, drop this. It can do nobody any good. You came up here—didn't you?—because you were disturbed by the same sound that disturbed me. Somebody shooting one of those damned things. And we both know that nobody practises archery in the small hours just for fun.

'There is the possibility of a bet, sir. Gentlemen have their peculiar ways.'

'For heaven's sake, man, stop behaving like a stage butler. You know, even better than I do, that there's some devilry afoot in this place.'

'Yes . . . yes, I do.' Frape passed a hand over his forehead, like a man who gives up. 'Only, I must—'

At this moment the creak of a door made itself heard from the far end of the gallery. Appleby was about to turn towards the noise, when Frape restrained him.

'Don't turn round,' he said in a low voice. 'I can see—without being detected as doing so. I think somebody is watching us through the door.' He began to fiddle with the door-handle of the ascham. 'Yes,' he said in a louder tone. 'The catch is defective, sir, and so the door has simply been blowing to and fro. There is always a draught in the gallery.' Once more he lowered his voice. 'He's opened it wider. It's Mr Trevor. He's shut it again. He's gone.'

'You mean to say'—now Appleby did turn round—'that this fellow Trevor has come up here, peered in at us in a furtive manner, and made himself scarce again?'

'Yes, sir. And it is certainly another indication that things are not as they ought to be.'

'Quite so. And the question is, where do we go from here? Have you any idea where we might find that fellow Jolly?'

'In his bed, I suppose.'

'Jolly's bed hasn't been slept in. Were you aware of any coming and going about the place after the company broke up last night?'

'I have an impression, sir, that there was some talking going on in the library until about midnight. Whether Mr Jolly was concerned, I don't know. But would I be correct in assuming that you are aware of something seriously to his disadvantage?'

'That puts it mildly, Frape. The man's a professional criminal.'

'Then I suggest that he may have left the Castle. Mr Darien-Gore may have detected him in some design that has resulted in his beating a hasty retreat. It would be perfectly possible. The wind has dropped, and I think there has been no more snow.' As he said this, and as if to confirm his impression, Frape crossed over to a window.

'It's a possibility, certainly,' Appleby said. 'And I wonder—'

'Sir'—Frape's voice had changed suddenly—'will you be so good as to step this way?'

Appleby did so, and found himself looking obliquely down into the moonlit inner bailey. It was a moment before he realised the small change that had taken place in the scene. Between the well and one side of the surrounding courtyard there was a line of tracks in the snow.

'Mr Darien-Gore's binoculars, sir. He keeps a pair in the gallery.'

Appleby took the binoculars and focused. There could be no doubt about what he saw. A line of heavy footprints led straight to the well. There were none leading the other way.

'Ought I to rouse Mr Darien-Gore, sir?' Frape asked, as Appleby put down the binoculars and turned away from the window.

'Certainly you must.' Appleby moved across the gallery to

the great fireplace. 'And everybody else as well. But it will be rather a chilly occasion for them—particularly for the ladies. Would you say, Frape, that this fire could be blown up quickly?'

'Decidedly, sir. A little work with the bellows will produce a blaze in a few minutes.'

'Then this will be the best place in which to meet. You had better get on to the job. . . . But one moment.' Appleby held up a hand. 'You could not have been mistaken about the identity of the man peering in on us a few moments ago?'

'Certainly not. It was Mr Trevor.'

'Nor could you have had any motive for . . . deceiving me in the matter?'

'I quite fail to understand you, sir.'

'Do you think that Mr Trevor—if Mr Trevor it is—may have some reason for entering the gallery? Might he be outside that door still, hoping that we shall leave by the other one?'

'I can't imagine any reason for such a thing.'

'Can't you? Well, I propose to put it to the test, by going down the one staircase, through the hall, and up the other one now. You will stay here, please, blowing up the fire.'

'I don't see that—'

'Frape, you're far from being in the dark about what we're up against. Please do as I say.'

This time, Appleby waited for no reply, but left the gallery by the door beside the target, and ran downstairs, playing his torch before him. As an outflanking move it seemed a forlorn hope, but in fact it was startlingly successful. When, a couple of minutes later, he returned breathlessly into the gallery by the other door, he was hustling before him a figure who had in fact still been lurking there. It wasn't Charles Trevor. It was Robert Darien-Gore.

'All right, Frape,' Appleby said. 'Get everybody in here. But give them a few minutes to get dressed—and get dressed yourself.' He turned to Robert, who was wearing knicker-bockers and a shooting-jacket. 'You mustn't mind my staying as I am,' he said. 'It might be a mistake if you and I were to waste any time in beginning to work this thing out.'

VII

'Good God!' General Strickland said, and put down the binoculars. He was the last of the company to have accepted Appleby's invitation to scrutinise the inner bailey. 'The fellow walked deliberately out and killed himself. And in that hideous way.'

'It isn't,' Mrs Strickland asked, 'some . . . some abominable joke? He can't, for instance, have tiptoed back again in his own prints in the snow?'

'I'm afraid not.' Appleby, who was planted before what was now a brisk fire, shook his head. 'Robert Darien-Gore was good enough to accompany me down to the inner bailey a few minutes ago. We didn't go right out to the well—I want those tracks photographed before any others are made —but I satisfied myself—professionally, if I may so express it —that nobody can have come back through that snow. Whatever the tracks tell, they don't tell that.'

'The snow on the parapet,' Trevor said rather hoarsely, '—on the low wall, I mean, round the well—seems to have prints at one point too.'

'Precisely. And the picture seems very clear. There is one person, and one person only, missing from the castle now— a chance guest like myself: the man Jolly. Whether deliberately or by accident, he has . . . gone down the well. And I believe you all know what *that* means.'

'By accident?' Strickland asked. 'How could it be an accident?'

'I can't see how it could possibly be,' Judith Appleby said.

'No sane man would take it into his head to go out in the middle of the night—'

'He was a bit tight,' Jasper Darien-Gore said. 'I don't know if that's relevant, but it's a fact. Frape—you noticed it?'

'Most emphatically, sir. Although not incapacitated, the man was undoubtedly tipsy.'

'He must have decided to go back to his car.' Prunella Darien-Gore broke in with this. 'He thought he'd go outside the castle, and he went blundering through the snow—'

'It's not impossible,' Appleby said. 'Only it doesn't account for Jolly's climbing up on the lip of the well. Face up to that, and suicide is the only explanation. Or it would seem to be. But Mr Robert has another theory. You may judge it bizarre, but it fits the facts. Frape, do you remember saying something to me about a bet?'

'Yes, sir. It was in a slightly different connection. But the point is a very relevant one.'

'And I think you remarked that gentlemen have their peculiar ways?'

'I did, sir. I trust the observation was not impertinent.'

'According to Mr Robert, Mr Darien-Gore himself happened to recount at the dinner-table some legend or superstition about the well. It was to the effect that notable good luck will be won by any man who makes his way to the well at midnight, stands on its wall, and invocates the moon.'

'Does *what*?' General Strickland exclaimed. 'Some pagan nonsense, eh? God bless my soul!'

'It's perfectly true.' Jasper spoke slowly. 'I did spin that old yarn. And I can imagine some young man—a subaltern, or undergraduate, for instance—who might have received it as a dare. But not that fellow Jolly. He wasn't the type. It doesn't make sense.'

'Unfortunately, something further happened.' Appleby still stood in front of the fireplace; he might almost have been on guard before it. 'Mr Robert—so he tells me—made

43

some sort of wager with Jolly. Or perhaps he did no more than vaguely suggest a wager. He was trying, as I understand the matter, to entertain the man—who was not altogether in his element among us. Have I got it right?'

Most of the company were standing or sitting in a wide circle round Appleby. But Robert had sat down a little apart. He might have been taking up, quite consciously, an isolated and alienated pose—rather suggestive of young Hamlet at the court of his uncle Claudius. He had remained silent so far. But now he replied to Appleby's challenge.

'Yes,' he said. 'Just that. I said something about a bottle of Jasper's Margaux if Jolly could tell me in the morning that he had done this stupid and foolhardy thing. I repent it bitterly. In fact, I hold myself responsible for the man's death.'

'Come, come,' General Strickland said kindly. 'That's a morbid view, my dear Robert. You were doing your best to entertain the fellow, and what has happened couldn't be foreseen.'

'It isn't the truth! It can't be!' Prunella had sprung to her feet in some ungovernable agitation. 'He still wasn't that sort of man. He was calculating . . . cold. I hated him.' She turned to her husband. 'Robert—you're not hiding something . . . shielding somebody?'

'Prunella, for God's sake control yourself.' Robert made what was almost a weary gesture. 'It's a queer story, I know. But there it is.'

'Which puts the matter in a nutshell.' Appleby had taken a single step forward, and the effect was to make him oddly dominate the people in the long gallery. 'It's a queer story. But it's conceivable. And there isn't any other in the field. Not unless we have a few more facts. As it happens, we *have* more facts. The first of them is a bow-shot in the night. Strickland, would you mind stepping through that door at the end of the gallery, and bringing in anything you find hidden behind it?'

General Strickland did as he was asked, and came back carrying a bow.

'It's a bow,' he said—a shade obviously. 'And there's an arrow there too.'

'Precisely. And somebody was concerned to return them to the ascham here within the last hour. Frape appears to be convinced that that person was Mr Trevor. So perhaps Mr Trevor somehow lured Jolly up on the lip of the well, and then—so to speak—shot him into it. One moment!' Appleby stopped Trevor on the verge of some outburst. 'Another fact is this: Jolly was, to my knowledge, a professional blackmailer. And his arrival here wasn't fortuitous; it was designed. Moreover—but this is conjecture rather than fact—he and Mr Trevor were not entirely unknown to each other—'

'*That's* true.' Charles Trevor was a very frightened man. 'I had an . . . an encounter with Jolly in the past. Suddenly coming upon him again was a great shock. But it wasn't—'

'Very well. Suppose Frape didn't see Mr Trevor peering through that door. Supposing he was concerned to shield—'

'Of course Frape saw *me*. And then *you* discovered me. And now Strickland has discovered the bow and arrow.' Robert Darien-Gore got these statements out in a series of gasps. 'I haven't been sleeping. Last night I knew it wasn't even worth while going to bed. So I passed the time repairing one of the horns of that bow, and feathering an arrow. Then I brought them back here.' Looking round the company, Robert met absolute silence. 'I give you all my word of honour as a gentleman,' he said, 'that I did not shoot Jolly.'

There was another long silence, broken only by an inarticulate sound from Prunella.

'We can accept that,' Appleby said gently. 'But you killed him, all the same.'

'Jolly came to Gore Castle in the way of trade,' Appleby said. 'His own filthy trade. He had papers he was going to

45

sell—at a price. I don't know what story these papers tell. But it is the story that failed to see the light of day when Robert Darien-Gore had to leave the army. Jolly, I may say, made a sinister joke to me. He said he knew when he'd been given enough; he knew just how much he could take. He was wrong.'

'This must stop.' Jasper Darien-Gore spoke with an assumption of authority. 'If there is matter for the police to investigate, then the local police must be summoned in a regular way. Sir John, I consider that you have no standing in this matter. And it is an abuse—'

'You are quite wrong, sir.' Appleby looked sternly at his host. 'I am the holder of a warrant card, like any other officer of the police. And on its authority I propose to make an arrest on a specific charge. Now, may I go on?'

'For God's sake do!' Prunella cried out. 'I can't stand more of this . . . I can't stand it!'

'My dear,' Mrs Strickland said, and went to sit beside her.

'Strickland—take the binoculars again, will you? Look at the keep. Got it? What strikes you about it?'

'Chiefly the scaffolding round it, I'd say.'

'Windows?'

'There are narrow windows all the way up—lighting a spiral staircase, I seem to remember.'

'Glazed?'

'No.'

'Imagine a skilled archer near ground-level on the near side of the bailey. Could he get an arrow through one of those windows?'

'I suppose he could. First shot, if he was first class.'

'And on a flight that would pass over the well?'

'Certainly.'

'That was what happened. That was the bow-shot I heard and Frape heard. The arrow carried a line—by means of which somebody in the keep could draw a strong nylon cord across the bailey, something more than head-high above the well.' Appleby turned to Robert. 'You had already killed Jolly—simply with an arrow employed as a dagger, I rather think. He was a meagre little man. You carried the body to the well, pitched it in, mounted the lip—and returned across the bailey on the cord. For a climber, it wasn't a particularly difficult feat. Then the line was released at the other end, swung like a skipping rope until it fell near one of the flanking walls, and drawn gently back through the snow. There will be virtually no trace of it. It only remained to return the bow to the ascham here. The bow and one arrow. The second missing arrow is . . . with Jolly, I rather think.'

'You know too much.' Robert Darien-Gore had been sitting hunched in a chair, his right hand deep in the pocket of his shooting jacket. Now he sprang to his feet, brought out his hand, and hurled something in the direction of Appleby, which flew past him and into the fireplace. Then the hand went back again, and came out holding something else. The crack of a pistol shot reverberated in the gallery as Robert crashed to the floor.

'*By God—he's dead!*' Like a flash, Jasper had been on his knees beside his brother. But now he rose, dazed and staggering—and with the pistol in his hands. He came slowly over to Appleby. 'I think,' he said, 'my brother is . . . dead. Will you . . . see?'

Appleby took a couple of steps forward—and as he did so Jasper dived behind him. What Robert had hurled into the fireplace was Jolly's pocket-book; it had missed the fire, and lay undamaged. Jasper grabbed it just as Appleby turned, and made to thrust it into the heart of the flame. Appleby knocked up his arm, and the pocket-book went flying across the gallery. Jasper eluded Appleby's grasp, vaulted a settee with the effortlessness of a young athlete in training, retrieved the pocket-book, and turned round to face the company. He still had Robert's pistol in his hand.

'Don't move,' he said. 'Don't any of you move.'

'This is foolish,' Appleby said quietly. 'Foolish and useless. Your brother is indeed dead. And his last day's work has been to involve you in murder. You knew nothing about Jolly when he arrived—except that you distrusted him. But Robert made you receive him as a guest, and by dinner-time Robert had persuaded you to his plot. Your own first part in it was to concoct that legend about the well. But your main part was to be in the keep when the arrow arrived. You face a charge of murder, just as your brother would have done. Nothing is to be gained by waving a pistol.'

'All of you get back from that fire—now.' With raised pistol, Jasper took a pace towards Appleby. In his other hand he raised the pocket-book. 'What I hold here, I burn. After that, we can talk.'

'I'm sorry, Darien-Gore, but it won't do. Before you burn those papers, you'll have shot a policeman in the course of his duty. And if—'

'Permit me, sir.' Frape had stepped forward. He walked past Appleby and advanced upon his employer. 'It will be best, sir, that you should give me the gun.'

'Stand back, Frape, or I shoot.'

'As Sir John says, sir, it won't do. So, with great respect, I must insist.' And Frape put out a steady arm and took the pistol from his employer's hand. 'Thank you, sir. I am obliged to you.'

For a fraction of a second Jasper looked merely bewildered. Then, as Appleby again advanced upon him, he turned and ran from the gallery.

'Frape—help me to get him.' Instinctively, Appleby addressed first the man who had proved himself. He was already running down the gallery as he called over his shoulder. 'Strickland, Trevor—he must be stopped.'

VIII

The chase through Gore Castle took place in the first light
of a bleak winter dawn. Judith Appleby, who had followed
the men, was to remember it as a confusion of panting and
shouting, with ill-identified figures vanishing down vistas that
were composed sometimes of stately rooms in unending
sequence, sometimes of narrow defiles through forbidding
mediaeval masonry. It was the kind of pursuit that may
happen in nightmare: in one instant hopelessly at fault, and
in the next an all but triumphant breathing down the hunted
man's neck.

They were in the open—plunging and kicking through
snow. Suddenly, in front of Jasper as he rounded a corner,
there seemed to be only a high blank wall. But he ran straight
at it; a buttress appeared; in the angle of this stood a ladder,
steeply pitched. Appleby and Frape were at its foot seconds
after Jasper's heels had vanished up it; but even as they
were about to mount it it came down past their heads. As
they struggled to set it up again Judith could see that Jasper,
with a brief respite won, was crouched down on a narrow
ledge, and fumbling in a pocket. With trembling hands he
produced a box of matches—and then Jolly's fatal pocket-
book. From this he pulled out a first sheet of paper, crumpled
it, struck a match. But the match—and then a second and a
third—went out. And now the ladder was in place again.
There was no time for another attempt. Clutching the
pocket-book, Jasper rose and ran on. He vanished through a
low archway. He had gained the keep.

It was almost dark inside. Judith was now abreast of her
husband. As they paused to accustom themselves to the
gloom, Jasper's voice came from somewhere above.

'Are you there, Appleby? I don't advise the climb.'

'Darien-Gore, come down—in the name of the law.'

'This is my keep, Appleby. It was to defy the law—didn't I tell you?—that my ancestors built it long ago.'

The last words were almost inaudible, for Jasper was climbing again. They followed. Perpendicular slits of light spiralled downwards and past them as they panted up the winding stair. Quite suddenly, there was open sky in front of them, and against it Jasper's figure in silhouette. In front of him was a criss-cross of scaffolding. One aspect of it they had seen from other angles already : a wooden plank, thrusting out into vacancy for some feet—and startlingly suggestive of a spring-board. Beyond it, the eye could only travel vertiginously down . . . to the inner bailey, the well, the single set of prints across the snow.

Jasper turned for a moment. They could see his features dimly, and then—very clearly—that he was holding up the pocket-book to them in a gesture of defiance. He thrust it into a pocket, turned away, measured his distance, and ran. It was not a jump; it was the sort of dive that earns a high score in an Olympic pool. In a beautiful curve Jasper Darien-Gore rose, pivoted in air, plunged, diminished in free fall, and vanished (as they ceased to be able to bear to look) into the well.

And from behind them came the breathless voice of General Strickland :

'Good God, Appleby! Jasper didn't better that one when he gained a Gold for England in '36.'

POLTERGEIST

'A u n t J e s s i c a h a s a poltergeist,' Judith Appleby
said, as she watched her husband pour drinks. John had got
home from Scotland Yard after a hard day. High-powered
criminals were very much abroad in the land, and he had
conferred at length with half a dozen of his most major
officers about one large-scale villainy or another. He deserved
to be entertained with a little relaxing family gossip.

'In that case your aunt had better keep a sharp eye on the
new kitchen-maid.' Appleby handed Judith her sherry.
'Better ring her up and tell her so.'

'There isn't a new kitchen-maid. In fact kitchen-maids are
no longer heard of.'

'In the kind of household your Aunt Jessica runs to I'll
bet they are, although there may be a new name for them.
In any event, what the old lady must look out for is an
adolescent girl—preferably of worse than indifferent educa-
tion, and necessarily of hysterical temperament. If poltergeists exist, it's almost invariably when some such young
person is around that they get busy toppling the furniture
and chucking the china about the house. If they don't exist,
one has to conclude that dotty girls can develop surprising
skill in putting on such turns themselves. The subject is a
perplexed one. Para-psychologists are by no means in
agreement about it.'

'Isn't that because there's often such a mix-up of straight
fraud and genuinely inexplicable happenings?' Judith felt
she was at least getting John's mind off bank-robberies and
rapes and muggings. 'For instance, a man finds he can make
billiard balls roll about the table simply by glaring at them.

Then he is investigated by professors and people who turn out to be an unsympathetic crowd. His powers begin to desert him in these new conditions, and soon he is doing it with magnets or something hidden up his shirt-sleeves.'

'I've never heard of the billiard-balls man.'

'No more have I. I've made him up. But that sort of thing.'

'I agree that there have been plenty of such cases. The ladies known as physical mediums are the best documented of them. But it's more interesting when the thing operates the other way round. The professional stage illusionist makes a few passes, mutters some abracadabra, and the pretty girl in the box vanishes. It's done with mirrors, as everybody knows. Then one day he does it once too often, and the girl *really* vanishes, never to be seen or heard of again.'

'I've never heard of *that*, John.'

'Of course not. But—once more—that sort of thing. And now tell me more about your poor aunt's predicament. I hope the manifestations are confined to the kitchen.'

'They're not. The poltergeist has managed to smash a white porcelain dish of the Liao dynasty. And that, you know, means a hundred years before the Norman Conquest.'

'Good God!' Appleby was genuinely shocked. 'Anything else of that order?'

'An eight-faceted vase of *mei-p'ing* shape. Underglaze blue with dragons in waves.'

'That would be Yüan—and I think I remember it. This must be stopped. Has the old lady called in the police?'

'She called in the vicar, and the vicar produced an ecclesiastical exorcist, specially licensed for the job by the Archbishop of Canterbury. There's been bell, book and candle stuff all over Anderton Place. But the poltergeist hasn't been incommoded so far.'

'Then the good Lady Parmiter must be persuaded to try the local constabulary after all—and not just as a last resort.' Appleby, far from amused, frowned at his untouched sherry.

'It's monstrous, Judith. A vast great country house, absolutely crammed with treasures waiting to be smashed to bits by some unfortunate child of disordered mind! And nothing done about it, you say, except in terms of clerical mumbo-jumbo? The old dear ought to be locked up.'

'Don't be so cockily rationalistic, John. Of course you're right about the treasures. Acres and acres of the things. But acres and acres of utter junk as well. Aunt Jessica's late husband was enormously wealthy. As a collector he was also as guileless and tasteless as they come. The result is that Anderton Place must be pretty well unique among the dwellings of men.'

'But does your aunt *know*? What's genuine and what's fake, and so on?'

'It's impossible to tell—but she certainly likes living with the old higgledy-piggledy effect perpetrated by my uncle. Loyalty to the deceased, perhaps. Her trustees must have accurate inventories based on adequate expertises made by museum people and so forth. The insurance position would be chaotic without that. But Anderton Place itself *is* chaotic, as you've seen for yourself.'

'Not so chaotic as it will be when this precious poltergeist is finished with it.'

'That's how it looks, I must say.' Judith Appleby glanced at her husband with caution, and confirmed herself in the view that he had been working far too hard. There were even dark rings under his eyes. 'Yes,' she said. 'And you're quite right. It *ought* to be stopped. Why not stop it?'

'What's that?'

'Aunt Jessica has a high regard for you—'

'Judith, are you suggesting that I take time off to run this blessed poltergeist to earth? The idea's absurd.'

'You said yourself she ought to call in the police. And if there's a policeman in the family—'

'More sherry? It's almost dinner-time.'

'John, dear, don't be evasive. And think of all that stuff.

Sung and T'ang and heaven knows what. And only poor old Aunt—'

'Poor old fiddlesticks. Your precious aunt is as formidable a dowager as any of her kind in England.'

'Don't you feel you could handle her?'

'Of course I could handle her.' As he uttered this boast Appleby caught his wife's eye and grinned. 'Oh, very well,' he said. And he reached out for the telephone beside him. 'I'll cancel things,' he said. 'Just for tomorrow, mind you. I can't play truant for longer than that.'

'The poltergeist may not last even that long with *you* on the job, darling.'

And with this very proper expression of confidence uttered, Judith Appleby went to see about the dinner.

It is well known that poltergeists, in common with other agents of the supernatural, frequently sulk when attracting the interest of persons sceptically inclined. Aunt Jessica's poltergeist may have regarded the Applebys not as sceptical but merely as open-minded; certainly it lost no time in showing that it remained in business. Appleby hadn't finished his polite inquiries about Lady Parmiter's health—indeed the butler who had announced the visitors hadn't left the drawing-room—when the unmistakable sound of breaking china announced the fact. From a high unglazed shelf crowded with the stuff a medium-sized jar had tumbled to the parquet floor and exploded like a fragmentation bomb.

Appleby strode over to the resulting small disaster and picked up a couple of the larger pieces. Although scarcely an expert on Oriental ceramics, he had no difficulty in identifying what had been destroyed. The Parmiter Collection—so enormous and so eccentrically miscellaneous—was the poorer by one of those nicely manufactured pots in which one buys preserved ginger at rather superior shops.

'Sometimes T'ang and sometimes Fortnum and Mason,'

he said rather grimly to Aunt Jessica. 'Your visitant must certainly be described as having catholic tastes.'

'As my dear husband himself had.' Aunt Jessica produced this odd rejoinder with dignity. She certainly wasn't at all an easy old lady.

'Yes, of course.' Appleby spoke absently. Taking the freedom of a fairly close relation, he had scrambled on a chair and was investigating the shelf from which the jar had fallen. It stood close to a high window of which the upper sash was open. Nobody had been looking that way when the thing happened. Beyond this, there was nothing to be remarked. He got down again, collected a brush and shovel from the fireplace, composedly swept up the bits and pieces, and deposited them in a waste-paper basket. Performing this more or less menial action appeared to put something further in his head. 'How many indoor servants have you got at present?' he asked.

'Fewer, certainly, than some years ago.' For a moment Lady Parmiter seemed to feel that this was as precise a computation as she could fairly be expected to arrive at. But then she tried harder. 'Seven,' she said, 'or eight? Not more than that.'

'I suppose you can just manage,' Judith said without irony. Unlike her husband, she had been accustomed to large establishments in youth. 'I take it they are all reliable, and have been with you for a good many years?'

'I fear not. The minds of domestic servants, Judith, are undeniably unsettled. I sometimes judge, too, that a nomadic habit is establishing itself among them. Their faces are frequently unfamiliar to me, so I think they must come and go. My housekeeper, Mrs Thimble, would tell you about that. I don't, of course, include Mrs Thimble in the eight. She is almost a companion to me in her humble way. Unfortunately she is absent for a few days, owing to some bereavement in her family.'

Appleby had betrayed some impatience during these

unhelpful remarks, and had received a warning glance from Judith. Now he tried again.

'I know,' he said, 'that you don't much care for the police. But you might—' He broke off, having been interrupted by a series of bumps and shudders, followed by a splintering crash, apparently from just outside the drawing-room. He ran to the door and threw it open. Anderton Place rejoiced in a very grand marble-sheathed hall and a correspondingly imposing marble staircase. The hall was now littered with the debris of an enormous wardrobe. Minor bits and pieces— the first to detach themselves from the tumbling monster— lay here and there on the stairs. The bizarre effect was enhanced by the fact that the wardrobe had apparently contained a very large collection of Victorian and Edwardian clothing. This, too, now lay all over the place.

'I was about to remark,' Appleby said calmly when the startled ladies had joined him, 'that two courses are possible. You might, Aunt Jessica, call in one of the big security firms. They would send you a few skilled people, in the guise of accountants or solicitors' clerks or indigent clergy deserving a country holiday—'

'Quite out of the question.' Lady Parmiter made no bones about this. 'I should regard anything of the sort as most objectionable.'

'Alternatively, there are highly reputable bodies devoted to the pursuit of psychical research. Archbishops and Prime Ministers have been among their active members from time to time. Their attitude is totally objective and disinterested, just as is that of any other learned society. They possess great experience alike in assessing the significance of genuine paranormal phenomena and in detecting imposture. If you cared—'

'I will have nothing to do with anything of the sort, John. Dear Adolphus would not have approved of it. Judith, is that not so?'

'Yes, Aunt Jessica, I suppose it is. But then Uncle

Adolphus was never up against a peculiarly destructive poltergeist.'

'There is the luncheon bell, my dear. Your uncle always liked an old-fashioned bell. I have had to instruct this new butler—whose name escapes me—to refrain from entering and announcing meals. And that reminds me. We shall not discuss these disturbing incidents before the servants. I hope the man has remembered the Andron-Blanquet. I recall it, John, as your favourite claret. Malign spirits may be at work. But at least they have made no attack upon the cellar.'

And Lady Parmiter, a spirited woman, led the way to her dining-room.

The meal was uneventful. Spoons and forks didn't tie themselves into knots, or take to the air and vanish. The only mishap was a minor one, when a young parlour-maid contrived to spill an uncomfortably hot potato into Judith's lap. Appleby found himself giving an eye to this girl. If she was a professional, it didn't seem to be at waiting at table. And to a trained sense her relationship to the anonymous butler was detectably odd. This might be taken to count against the view that she was the standard hysterical female of canonical poltergeist literature. Appleby rose from table with a dim theory stirring in his mind.

Then—again claiming family status—he took a prowl through Anderton Place alone. Even more than he remembered, it was a mad museum from cellars to attics. In the cellars there was plenty of that sound and modest claret; there was even more claret that was very rare indeed; there was also a bewildering amount of wine for which the late Lord Parmiter must have scoured every fifth-rate grocer's shop in the country. The attics were full of rubbish—some of it honest-to-God rubbish, and some of it fake furniture of the most pretentious sort. And every now and then one came on something which would have satisfied the most exacting

57

taste in the age of Louis Quatorze. The effect was a kind of security nightmare. It cried out for skilled pillage.

And so with the rest of the house. As the crazy Lord Parmiter had disposed everything, so was everything disposed now. It would take the entire staff of the British Museum a month's labour, one could feel, to separate the wheat from the chaff.

There were several further 'disturbing incidents' (as Aunt Jessica had termed them) while Appleby prowled. At one point a worthless but lethal bracket clock hurtled past Appleby's ear and smashed into a cabinet containing some decidedly precious Dresden china. The whole affair was clearly mounting to a crisis.

Back in the drawing-room, Appleby found that Judith had been trying to persuade her aunt to take drastic emergency action. She ought to send her entire staff away on board-wages, shut up the house, and leave merely a thoroughly reliable caretaker in charge. Appleby didn't think much of this plan. Nor—more conclusively—did Lady Parmiter. If the poltergeist really was a poltergeist (and on this she, too, professed an open mind) the result might merely be major disaster. More poltergeists might simply move in, and the last state of Anderton be worse than its first. Appleby agreed, or professed to agree. He had an alternative suggestion. The most experienced packers in London should be hastily brought in. Working under Lady Parmiter's direction, they could crate up everything of the first value for immediate removal to impregnable strong-rooms in the metropolis. Poltergeists were invariably confined to one stamping-ground. They wouldn't be able to follow.

Lady Parmiter turned this down too—but with a shift of ground. Such a proceeding would be abhorrent to the shade of dear Adolphus, and was therefore not to be entertained for a moment. It seemed an impasse. Appleby produced what seemed to be a final throw.

'But doesn't Anderton run to something like a strong-room of its own?' he asked. 'I seem to remember Judith's uncle speaking of something of the kind, and being rather proud of it.'

'We simply call it the safe, John, but it is in fact a large room and entirely burglar-proof. I always lock my dear mother's Queen Anne silver away in it when I have occasion to leave Anderton.'

'That's very prudent of you.' Appleby was wondering whether he could possibly bring this perverse old person to see reason. At least he mustn't give up without a further attempt. 'May I see it?' he asked. 'Your husband was extremely wise to have such a thing constructed. No great house should be without one.'

The request, thus framed, was well received. The Anderton strong-room looked tremendously impressive—and had looked just that for at least fifty years. Indeed, it might have been some triumph of metallurgical skill triumphantly displayed at the Great Exhibition at the Crystal Palace in 1851. If Appleby was amused at this outmoded affair he managed not to betray the fact.

'Look,' he said, '—couldn't we simply put everything that is really valuable in here? I'm sure Lord Parmiter would have approved. We have on our hands just the sort of situation he must have been envisaging when he ordered so spacious an affair. If what we're up against is simple human vandalism or madness, then we defeat it in this simple way. If it's something supernatural, we're at least no worse off than we are at present. Of course you're the only person who knows what's what; who can quickly pick out the really precious things from those which are to be classed as primarily of sentimental value. I honestly feel you should do this, Aunt Jessica. It's your duty as the guardian of all the marvellous things Lord Parmiter gathered together. And it can all be done this afternoon. You show us what, and the whole household can help with the stowing.'

Perhaps surprisingly, Lady Parmiter agreed to this plan at once. The undisturbed disposition of things at Anderton was very dear to her as one of the pieties of widowhood. She was a good Victorian, after all, and the impulse was the same as that which had prompted a more famous Widow to preserve intact the arrangements on her deceased Prince Consort's writing table. On the other hand she had a shrewd sense of what things were worth, and no reason to believe that dear Adolphus would have smiled on the indiscriminate massacre of his wildly heterogeneous treasures.

The task was accomplished by a late dinner-time, the bewildered servants being directed (in the absence of the bereaved Mrs Thimble) by the butler without a name. Anderton didn't look all that denuded when the job was finished. All the same, objects worth many hundreds of thousands of pounds had been segregated and placed under lock and key. The poltergeist was thwarted—or so it was to be hoped.

The Applebys drove back to London in the dark—but not before Appleby himself had contrived a short private conversation with Lady Parmiter.

'Lucky your aunt turned out to know the stuff fairly well,' he said.

'Yes.'

'I doubt whether much that's really first-rate now remains outside that strong-room.'

'I suppose not.'

'You'd agree, Judith, that Aunt Jessica has been persuaded to do the rational thing?'

'Clearly she has—unless it really is a supernatural agency that's at work.'

'You'd also agree that what she has done is the *obvious* thing in the circumstances?'

'Well, yes. But I don't see—'

'The *predictable* thing?' It was almost in anxiety that

Appleby appeared to wait for his wife's acquiescence this time.

'Absolutely.'

'Then I think all's well. Yes, I'm pretty sure of it. By the way, just give a glance at the bedroom tomorrow. Your aunt's coming to stay with us.'

'To stay with us!'

'Oh, not for long. Just for two or three days. She's telling that butler tonight that she's coming to us in the morning.'

'How very odd! But at least we can get a good night's sleep first.'

'Very true. Just one telephone call, and I'll be ready for it.'

'A telephone call?'

'To the Thames Valley Constabulary, my dear. Anderton is on their territory—so I must liaise with them, as people now say.' And Appleby laughed softly as he swung the steering-wheel. 'I set the trap. They spring it.'

'All caught,' Appleby announced a couple of mornings later. 'Butler, phoney parlour-maid—'

'I recall remarking,' Lady Parmiter said, 'that servants tend to be rather unreliable nowadays.'

'Quite so—and in fact two more were in the pay of the gang. All small fry, of course, the butler included. Fortunately their bosses decided to be in at the kill. Our Thames Valley friends nicked the lot while they were happily treating your strong-room, Aunt Jessica, like a hunk of old cheese.'

'We had really done quite a lot of their work for them?' Judith asked.

'Just that. They count as top-ranking villains, but happen not to be all that clued up on the fine-art front. They could only have made a purely random haul by themselves. Hence the poltergeist, who made us work like mad doing all the sifting for them.'

'But John, what about the tumbling jar? That *did* look like the real thing.'

'Not to me. A little bladder on the end of a long tube passing through the window. Squeeze a bulb at the other end, and the trick's accomplished. You just pull the thing out through the window again, and there you are. Literally a trick. Every kid's conjuring-set includes a miniature version of the same thing.'

'I must go upstairs and pack at once.' Aunt Jessica announced this firmly. 'It would be the wish of dear Adolphus that the *status quo ante* at Anderton be restored forthwith. And Mrs Thimble must find me a new butler. His first task, my dear John, will be to pack up every bottle of Andron-Blanquet I still possess. And I needn't tell you where it will be despatched to.'

THE FISHERMEN

I N S C O T L A N D T R O U T - F I S H I N G, almost as much as deer-stalking and grouse-shooting, is an amusement for wealthy men. Appleby was not particularly wealthy. From a modest station he had risen to be London's Commissioner of Metropolitan Police—a mouthful which his children, accurately enough, had turned into better and briefer English as Top Cop.

Top Cop's job turning out, predictably, to be more purely administrative than was at all enlivening, Appleby had retired from it earlier than need be, and now lived as an unassuming country gentleman on a small estate in the south of England which was the property of his wife. This, very happily, had proved not incompatible with getting into odd situations from time to time. Sir John Appleby liked odd situations. As a country gentleman he also, of course, liked fishing.

So he had accepted Vivarini's invitation to bring a rod to Dunwinnie, although he didn't really know the celebrated playwright particularly well. Now here he was, cheek by jowl with four other piscatory enthusiasts in what had once been a crofter's cottage. Crofters, and all such humbly independent tillers of the soil, had almost vanished from this part of the Scottish Highlands. Whether in small patches or in large, the region had been turned into holiday terrain for those rich men.

Appleby didn't brood on this. At least the hunting-boxes and shooting-lodges were (like everything else) thin on the ground. From the cottage one saw only the river—a brawling flood interspersed with still-seeming pools, brown from the

63

peat and with trout enough—with an abandoned lambing-hut on its farther bank and then the moorland that stretched away to the remote line of the Grampians. Dr Johnson, Appleby remembered, had once surveyed this scene and disliked it. *A wide extent of hopeless sterility*, he had written down. *Quickened only with one sullen power of useless vegetation.* That had been the heather.

There was a brushing sound in the heather now. Appleby looked up from his task of gutting fish for supper, and saw that his host was returning. Vivarini had been the last to leave the water. He seemed to be a keen angler. In his stained waders, Balmoral bonnet festooned with dry-flies, and with his respectably battered old creel, he certainly looked the part. But perhaps the playwright had enough of the actor in him for that. Snobbery and expensive rural diversions are inextricably tied up together in Britain, and in pursuit of some elusive social status men will go fox-hunting who in their hearts are terrified at the sight of a horse. Perhaps Vivarini with his costly stretch of trout-stream was a little like that.

Very rightly, Appleby felt mean at harbouring this thought, particularly as Vivarini looked so far from well. Even in the twilight now falling like an elfin gossamer over these haunted lands one could distinguish that about the man. Perhaps it was simply that he was under some sort of nervous strain. Appleby knew nothing about his London way of life, but there could well be things he wanted to get away from. A set-up like this at Dunwinnie—a small all-male society gathered for a secluded holiday on a bachelor basis—might well have been planned as wholesome relief by a man rather too much involved in something altogether different.

'Cloud coming up,' Vivarini said, 'and that breeze from the west stiffening. Makes casting tricky. I decided to stay with Black Gnat, by the way.' He indicated the fly still on the end of his line. 'A mistake, probably. Not sultry enough, eh?'

Clifford Childrey, ensconced with a three-day-old copy of the *Scotsman* on a bench beside the cottage door, glanced up—not at Vivarini but at Appleby—and then resumed his reading. He was Vivarini's publisher. A large and ruddy outdoor man, he had no need whatever to look a part.

'You deserve a drink, Vivarini,' Appleby said.

'Not so much as you do, sweating away as cook. I'll see to it. Sherry, I suppose? And you, Cliff?'

'Sherry.' Childrey momentarily lowered his newspaper. 'Don't know about the other two. They've gone downstream to bathe.'

'Right. I do like this American make.' Vivarini had leant his rod against the cottage's low thatched roof. 'No more than five ounces to the six feet. Flog the water all day with it.'

'Umph.' This response came from behind the *Scotsman*, which had been raised again. But it was tossed to the ground when Vivarini had entered the cottage. 'No need to be supercilious,' Childrey said.

'I've been nothing of the kind.' Appleby was amused at the charge. 'And if "umph" isn't supercilious, I don't know what is.'

'Well, well—Freddie Vivarini and I have been chums for a long time.' Childrey chuckled comfortably. 'A damned queer lot writers are, Appleby. I've spent my life trying to do business with them. Novelists are the worst, of course, but dramatists run them close. Always getting things up and trying out roles. What they call *personas*, I suppose. Thing-amies, really. Chimeras.'

'You mean chameleons.'

'That's right. No reliable personal identity. Shelley said something about it. Right up his own street.'

'Keats. You think our host is playing at being a sportsman?'

'Oh, at that and lots of other things. What he's run on all his life has been folding up on him. Unsuccessful literary man.'

'Unsuccessful?'

'Of course he's made a fortune. But that's what he's taken to calling himself. You're meant to regard it ironically. Uneasy joke, all the same.' Childrey checked himself and got to his feet, perhaps aware of talking too casually about his host. 'I'll start that grill for you,' he said. 'I see you'll need it soon.'

As if in one of Vivarini's own neat plays, Childrey's exit-line brought the subject of his late remarks promptly on-stage again. Vivarini was bearing glasses and a bottle which, even in the gloaming, could be seen as lightly frosted. The cottage was not wholly comfortless. Warmth was laid on for chilly evenings, and there was hot water and a refrigerator and a compendious affair for cooking any way you liked, all served by a few cylinders of butane trundled across the moor on a vehicle like a young tank. Not that their actual culinary regime wasn't simple enough. Elderly Englishmen of the sort gathered at Dunwinnie rather enjoy pretending to be public-schoolboys still, toasting crumpets or bloaters before a study fire. Of course there are limits, and when it is a matter of a glass of dry sherry or opening a bottle of hock, they don't expect the stuff to reach their palate other than at the temperature it should. Nor do they care to couch in straw. Appleby was just reflecting that the cottage's bunks had certainly come from an expensive shop when he became aware that his host, uncorked bottle in hand, was laughing cheerfully.

'I heard the old ruffian,' Vivarini said. 'Trying out roles, indeed! Well, what if I am?'

'What, indeed. I myself shall remain grateful to you. This is a delightful spot.'

'My dear Appleby, how nice of you to say so. But I do enjoy fishing, as a matter of fact. And—do you know?—as far as renting the cottage and this stretch of river goes, it was actually one of these chaps who egged me on. Positively ran me into it! But I won't say which.' Vivarini was laughing again—although with the effect, Appleby thought, of a man not wholly at ease. 'No names, no pack-drill. Ah, here come Mervyn and Ralph.'

Appleby couldn't afterwards remember—not even with a dead body to prompt him—who at the supper table had introduced the topic of crime. Perhaps it had been Ralph Halberd, since Halberd was one of that not inconsiderable number of millionaires to have suffered the theft of some enormously valuable pictures. This might have given Halberd an interest at least in burglars, although his line (outside owning shipping lines and luxury hotels) was a large if capricious patronage of artists expressing themselves in mediums more harmless than thermal lances and gelignite. Perhaps it had been Mervyn Gryde. Gryde wrote theatrical notices for newspapers (being dignified with the style of dramatic critic as a result), and the kind of plays he seemed chiefly to favour were, to Appleby's mind, so full of violence and depravity that crime must be supposed his natural element. Or it might have been Vivarini himself. Certainly it had been he who, exercising a host's authority, had insisted upon Appleby's recounting his own part in certain criminal *causes célèbres*. But it had been left to Childrey, towards the end of the evening, to insist with a certain flamboyance on toasting the retired Metropolitan Commissioner as the finest detective intelligence in Britain. The hock, Appleby thought, was a great deal too good for the toast; it had in fact been Halberd's contribution to the housekeeping and was quite superb. But he acknowledged the compliment in due form, and not long afterwards the company decided to go to bed.

Rather to his surprise, Appleby found himself obscurely relieved that the day was over. Everyone had been amiable enough. But had something been stirring beneath the talk, the relaxed gestures, the small companionable-seeming silences? As he dropped to sleep he found himself thinking of the deep still pools into which the Dunwinnie tumbled here and there on its hurrying and sparkling scramble towards the sea. Beneath those calm surfaces, whose only movement seemed to be the lovely concentric ripples from a rising trout, a strong current flowed.

He had a nightmare, a thing unusual with him. Perhaps it was occasioned by one of the yarns he had been inveigled into telling at the supper table of his early and sometimes perilous days in the C.I.D. In his dream he had been pursuing gunmen down dark narrow corridors—and suddenly it had been the gunmen who were pursuing him. They caught him and tied him up. And then the chief gunman had advanced upon him with a long whip and cracked it within an inch of his face. This was so unpleasant that Appleby, in his nightmare, told himself that here was a nightmare from which he had better wake up. So he woke up—not much perturbed, but taking thought, as one does, to remain awake until the same disagreeable situation was unlikely to be waiting for him.

The wind had risen and its murmur had joined the river's murmur, but inside the cottage there wasn't a sound. The single-storey building had been remodelled for its present purpose, and now consisted, like an ill-proportioned sandwich, of a large living-room in the middle, with a very small bedroom at each end. The bedrooms contained little more than two bunks set one above the other. Childrey and Halberd shared one of these cabin-like places, and Appleby and Vivarini had the other. Gryde slept on a camp-bed in the living-room. These dispositions had been arrived at, whimsically, by drawing lots.

Appleby turned over cautiously, so as not to disturb Vivarini underneath him. Vivarini didn't stir. And Appleby suddenly knew he wasn't there. It was a simple matter of highly developed auditory alertness. Nobody was breathing, however lightly, in the bunk below.

The discovery ought not to have been worth a thought. A

68

wakeful Vivarini might have elected for a breath of moor-land air. Or he might have been prompted to repair to the modest structure, some twenty yards from the cottage, known as the jakes. Despite these reflections, Appleby slipped quietly down from his bunk.

It was dark, then suddenly not dark, then dark again. But nobody had flashed a light. Outside, the sky must be a huddle of moving cloud, with a moon near the full some-times breaking through. Vivarini's bunk was indeed un-occupied. Appleby picked up a torch and went into the living-room. Gryde seemed sound asleep—a little dark man, Appleby passingly told himself, coiled up like a snake. The door of the farther bedroom was closed, but the door giving direct on the moor was open. Appleby stepped outside, switching off the torch as he did so. He now knew why he was behaving in this way—like an alarmed nursemaid, he thought. It was because of what had happened in his dream.

He glanced up at the clouds, and in the same moment the moon again came serenely through. The Dunwinnie rose into visibility before him, like a sudden outpouring of hoarded silver on dark cloth. On the other bank the lambing-hut with its squat square chimney suggested some small humped creature with head warily erect. And something was moving there. Momentarily Appleby saw this as a human figure slipping out of the door. Then he saw that it was only the door itself, swinging gently on its primitive wooden pivot. But no sound came from across the softly chattering flood; no sound that could have transformed itself into another sound in Appleby's dream.

There were stepping-stones here, practicable enough for an active man. But they faded into darkness as Appleby looked; the moon had disappeared again. He had to switch on the torch or risk a ducking. He risked the ducking, although he could scarcely have told himself why he disliked the idea of being seen. When he reached the hut he reconnoitred the ground before it with a brief flicker close to the earth. He felt for the door and pushed it fully open; it had been firmly shut, he remembered, and with an old thirl-pin through the latch, the evening before. Now he was looking into deep darkness indeed. The hut was no more than a square stone box with a slate roof; it had a fireplace more for the needs of the ewes and lambs than their shepherd; and in one wall —he couldn't recollect which—there was a window which had been boarded up. Treading softly, he moved through the door and listened.

No sound. No glimmer of light. Nothing to alert a single sense—unless it was a faint smell of old straw, the ghost of a faint smell of carbolic, of tar. Then suddenly, and straight in front of him at floor level, there was an illusive suggestion of light. All but imperceptibly, the small glow grew; it was as if a stage electrician were operating a rheostat with infinite care. It grew to an oblong, with darkness as its frame. And now within the frame there was a picture, there was a portrait. It was the portrait of Vivarini—but something had happened to his forehead. It was Vivarini himself.

Appleby was on his knees, his ear to the man's chest, his fingers exploring through a sports-coat, a pyjama-jacket. His face close to the still face, he flashed his torch into unclosing eyes, saw uncontracting pupils. He turned his head, gazed upwards, and was looking at a square of dimly luminous cloud. Nothing more than the moon's reflected light filtering down the chimney had produced that moment of hideous melodrama. Vivarini himself at his typewriter, or pacing his study while dictating to his secretary, couldn't have done better. It was backwards into the rude fireplace that he had crashed, a bullet in his brain. And hence the crack of that ugly whip in the other dimension of dream.

Twenty minutes passed before Appleby re-entered the cottage. Arrived there, he didn't waste time. He gave Gryde a rough shake and rapped smartly on the closed bedroom door. Within seconds his three fellow-guests were around him, huddled in dressing-gowns, dazed and blinking.

'Vivarini is dead,' he said quietly. 'In the lambing-hut. Shot through the head.'

'My God—so he meant it!' This exclamation was Ralph Halberd's, and it was followed by a small silence.

'One of us,' Appleby went on, apparently unheeding, 'must get down to Balloch, and telephone for a doctor and the police. But something a shade awkward comes first.'

'Awkward?' It was Mervyn Gryde who repeated the word, and his voice had turned sharp.

'Well yes. Let me explain. Or, rather, let me take up what Halberd has just said.' Appleby turned to the millionaire. ' "*My God—so he meant it!*" Just what made you say that?'

'Because he told me. He confided in me. It was a fearful shock.' In the cold light of a hissing gas-lamp, Halberd, who normally carried around with him an air as of imposing boardrooms, looked uncertain and perplexed. 'On Tuesday —the day we arrived. It was because I happened to see him unpack this thing, and shove it under his shirts in that drawer over there. A pistol. It looked almost like a toy.'

'Vivarini said he was going to kill himself with it?'

'Not that, exactly. Only that he had thoughts of it, and couldn't bring himself not to carry the weapon round with him.'

'Did he give any reason?'

'No. It seemed to be implied that he was feeling discouraged. His plays—all those Comedies of Discomfiture, as he called them—are a bit outmoded, wouldn't you say?'

'Perhaps so. But, Halberd, did you take any steps? Even mention this to any of the rest of us?'

'I wish to God I had. But I thought he was putting on a turn.' The patron's indulgent scorn for the artist sounded for a moment in Halberd's tones. 'That sort of fellow is always dramatising himself. And people don't often kill themselves just because they're feeling discouraged.'

'That's certainly true. There are psychologists who maintain that suicide never happens except on top of a clinically recognisable depressive state. An exaggeration, perhaps, but no more than that. But here's my point. Whatever Vivarini said to you, Halberd, he can't have made away with himself. I found no weapon in that hut.'

There was a long silence in the cottage.

'That's just according to one witness—yourself—who was the first man on the scene.' Gryde's voice was sharper still. And with a curiously reptilian effect, his tongue flickered out over dry lips.

'Exactly. You take my point.' Appleby smiled grimly. 'Anybody can tell lies. But let's see if there's a revolver under those shirts now.'

Watched by the others, Appleby made a brief rummage. No weapon was revealed.

'I may have killed him,' Halberd said slowly. 'And made up a stupid story about suicide, which the facts disprove.'

'Certainly you may.' Appleby might have been discussing a hand at bridge. 'But you're not going to be the only suspect.'

'Obviously not.' Childrey spoke for the first time. The least agitated of Appleby's companions, he might have been a rosy infant doubly-flushed from sleep. 'Nor are we—the four of us here—characters in a sealed-room mystery. Why the lambing-hut? Why did Vivarini go over there secretly in the night? To meet somebody unknown to us, one may suppose—and somebody who turned out not to care for him.'

'It might still have been one of ourselves,' Appleby said. 'But may I come back to the business of going for help? I'm thinking of the weapon. If one of us killed Vivarini, he may then have had enough time to get quite a distance across the moor and back for the purpose of hiding the gun where no search will ever find it. On the other hand, one of us may have it on his person, or in a suitcase, at this moment. Whichever of us goes for help must certainly be searched first. Or perhaps all of us. Do you agree? Good. I'll search each of you in turn—over there in that bedroom—and then one of you can search me.'

'I'll come first,' Childrey said easily. 'But behind that closed door. Less shaming, eh?'

Appleby's was a very rapid frisking. 'By the way,' he asked at the end of it, 'have you any notion how this fishing-party originated? You didn't by any chance suggest it to Vivarini, or in any way put him up to it?'

'Lord, no! Came as a complete surprise to me. We'd been on bad terms, as a matter of fact.'

'I'm sorry to hear it. Send in Halberd.'

Five minutes later, they were all in the living-room again. In another ten, the whole place had been searched.

'No gun,' Appleby said. 'But another lie—or the appearance of it. Vivarini told me one of you had egged him on to organise this little fishing-party. But each of you denies it.'

'All according to you,' Gryde said.

'Yes, indeed. I'm grateful to you for so steadily keeping me in mind. And now, who goes to telephone? It's at least five miles. I suggest we draw lots.'

'No. I'm going to go.' It was Childrey who spoke. 'Trekking over the moors in darkness is my sort of thing. I'll just get into a jacket and trousers.'

'The cunning criminal makes good his escape,' Gryde said. 'But it's all one to me.' He turned to Appleby. 'While Cliff is louping over the heather—I believe that's the correct Scots word—I suggest we open a bottle of whisky and have a nice friendly chat.'

It didn't prove all that friendly. Childrey's, it struck Appleby, had been the genuinely genial presence in the fishing-party; now, when he had gone off with long strides through a darkness with which the moon had ceased to struggle, the atmosphere in the cottage deteriorated sharply.

'Odd that Vivarini should have made *you* that confidence,

Ralph.' Gryde said this after the whisky bottle had clinked for a second time against his glass. 'And odd that he asked you here. Wanted to make it up with you, I suppose. Tycoons make ugly enemies.'

'What the devil do you mean?' Halberd had sat bolt upright.

'And it's going to be awkward for that girl. He'd miscalculated, hadn't he? Thought she was just one of your notorious harem, no doubt, and that you wouldn't give a damn. Actually, you were ludicrously in love with her. Not unusual, once a man has reached the age of senile infatuation. Everybody was talking about it, you know. And I'm surprised you came.'

'One might be surprised that cheerful idiot Childrey came.' Halberd had controlled himself with an effort in face of Gryde's sudden and astonishing assault. 'He told me that *he* had been on poor terms with Freddie. And, for that matter, what about yourself, Mervyn? I believe—'

'I don't filch other men's trollops.'

'You certainly don't. What you'd filch—'

'One moment.' Appleby had set down his glass—and he plainly didn't mean to take it up again. 'If we're to have this sort of thing—and experience tells me it may be inevitable— it had better be with *some* scrap of decency. No venom.'

'Venom is Mervyn Gryde's middle name.' Halberd reached for the bottle, but glanced at Appleby and thought better of it. 'Read the stuff he writes about any play in which the *dramatis personae* aren't a bunch of sewer rats. Read some of the things he's recently said about Freddie. He had his knife in Freddie. You'd suppose some hideous private grudge.' Halberd turned directly to the dramatic critic. 'How you can have had the forehead to accept an invitation from the poor devil beats me, Snaky Merv. That's what they called him at Cambridge long ago, you know.' This had the character of an aside to Appleby. 'Snaky Mervyn Gryde.'

'I'm afraid,' Appleby said drily, 'that I can't contribute

much to these amiable exchanges. I don't know a great deal about our late host. But of course—as you, Gryde, will be quick to point out—you have only my word for it. What I do see is that this party is revealing itself as having been organised by way of sinking differences and making friends again. And it hasn't had much luck. One result has been that, in your two selves, it brought here a couple of men with an undefined degree of animus against Vivarini. Perhaps Childrey has been a third. Can either of you explain what Childrey meant by telling me he'd been on bad terms with Vivarini?'

'I can, because Freddie told me. Not that you'll believe me.' Gryde, having apparently seen danger in too much whisky, was chain-smoking nervously, so that he was like some small dark devil risen from a nether world amid mephitic vapours. 'Childrey had refused to do a collected edition of Freddie's plays. And Freddie had found out it was because he was planning something of the sort for a rival playwright. Freddie was furious.'

'I can certainly believe that. But it's scarcely a reason why Childrey should murder Vivarini. Rather the other way about.'

'True enough.' Gryde laughed shrilly. 'But Freddie believed he was on the verge of exposing Childrey in some disreputable sharp practice about it all. He said he could wreck his good name as a publisher, and that he meant to do it.'

'And had meantime invited him to this friendly party? It's an uncommonly odd tale.'

'I said you wouldn't believe me.'

'On the contrary.' Appleby's smile was bleak. 'I'm inclined to believe that the dead man told you just what you say he did.'

'Thank you very much.' It wasn't without looking disconcerted that Gryde said this. 'And where the deuce do we go from here?'

'Exactly!' Halberd had got up and was restlessly pacing the room to the sound of a flip-flap of bedroom slippers. 'Where the deuce—and all the damned to boot.'

'We wait for the local police,' Appleby said. 'No doubt they will clear the matter up quickly enough.'

'Stuff and nonsense!' There was sudden violence in Halberd's voice. 'And I don't see this as an occasion for superior Scotland Yard irony, Appleby. The rotten business is up to you.'

'Well, yes. And I'm sorry about the irony. As a matter of fact, I rather agree with you. And I can't complain. You have both been most communicative—about yourselves, and about each other, and about Childrey. Childrey, too, has made his little spontaneous contribution. I really confront an *embarrass de richesses*, so far as significant information goes. You have laboured as one man, I might say, to give it to me.'

'And just what do you mean by that?' Gryde asked sharply.

'Perhaps very little.' Appleby yawned unashamedly. 'One tends to talk at random in the small hours, wouldn't you say?' He stood up, and walked to the open door of the cottage. 'Lights in the lambing-hut,' he said. 'Childrey has made uncommonly good time. And here he is.'

'And here you are.' Clifford Childrey echoed Appleby's words as he stood in the doorway. 'I was beginning to think I'd dreamed up the whole lot of you. Too fantastic—this affair.'

'Is that,' Halberd asked, 'what the doctor and the local copper are saying?'

'I don't know about the copper. He's an experienced sergeant, settling in to a thorough search, and not saying much meanwhile. As for the sawbones, he's the nice old family-doctor type. Agrees, of course, that the poor devil has been stone dead for at least a couple of hours. Seems to be wondering whether he was dead first, and dragged into the hut second. Suspects something rigged, you might say. Position of the body, and so forth. Appleby, what do you say to that?'

'I certainly felt an element of the theatrical to be present. But other things were present, too.'

'Clues, do you mean?'

'Clues? Oh, yes—several. Enough, in fact, to admit of only one explanation of the mystery.'

Sir John Appleby glanced from one to another of three dumbfounded faces, as if surprised that his announcement had occasioned any effect at all.

'As it happens,' he said, 'there is rather a good reason why the local sergeant won't find them—the clues, that's to say. But, as he is going to spend some time in the hunt, I propose to while away a quarter of an hour by telling you about them. Do you agree?'

'You'll have your say, I think, whether we agree or not.' Halberd had sat down heavily. 'So go on.'

'Thank you. But, first, I'd like to ask you something. Does it strike you as at all odd that the three of you—each, apparently, with a rather large dislike of Vivarini—should have accepted his invitation to come here in this particular week?'

'He took a lot of trouble to arrange it,' Gryde said. Gryde's voice had gone from high-pitched to husky. 'Dates, and so forth.'

'And there was this let-bygones-be-bygones slant to it.' Perhaps because his night tramp had been exhausting, Childrey might have been described as almost pale.

'Just that,' Halberd said. 'Wouldn't have been decent to refuse. Rum sort of coincidence, all the same—the lot of us like this.'

'Coincidence?' Appleby said. 'The word is certainly worth holding on to. Vivarini, incidentally, was holding on to something. Literally so, I mean. I removed that something from

77

his left hand, and have it in my pocket now. I don't intend to be mysterious about it. It was the cord of the silk dressing-gown that Gryde is wearing at this moment.'

'That's another of your filthy lies!' Before uttering this, Gryde had clutched grotesquely at his middle. Even as he did so, Appleby had produced the missing object and placed it quietly on the table.

'Making a bit free with the evidence, aren't you?' Childrey asked. He might have spoken out of a benevolent wish to give Gryde a moment in which to recover himself.

'Dear me! Perhaps I am.' Appleby offered this piece of innocence with perfect gravity. 'As a matter of fact, I've done rather the same thing with what appears to be property —or the remains of property—of your own, my dear Childrey. If photostatic copies of papers with your firm's letter-head are to be regarded as your property, that's to say. You remember the little place we made to boil a kettle, down by the river, the other afternoon? I discovered that a small file of such papers had been burnt there. And no time ago at all; I could still blow a spark out of them. Might they conceivably have been awkward—even compromising—documents that Vivarini had managed to get copies of—fatally for him, as it has turned out?'

'It's true about that collected edition,' Childrey said abruptly. 'I declined to do it, simply because there wouldn't be anything like an adequate market for it. It is untrue that I behaved improperly. And the notion of my killing Vivarini in order to recover and destroy—'

'But there's something more.' Appleby had raised a hand in a civil request for silence. 'Just to the side of the door of the lambing-hut there happens to be a patch of caked mud. The first thing I found was a footprint in it. Not of a shoe, but of a bedroom-slipper—with a soft rubber sole which carries a diamond-shaped maker's device on the instep. Yes, Halberd, you are quite right. You are wearing that slipper now.'

78

'Well,' Gryde said maliciously, 'that's something the sergeant *will* find.'

'Actually, I'm afraid not.' Appleby looked properly conscience-stricken. 'I was rather clumsy, I'm afraid. I trod all over the thing.'

'Can we have some explanation of all this madness—including your own totally irresponsible conduct?' It had been after a moment of general stupefaction that Gryde had put this to Appleby.

'Why, certainly. You all had a bit of a motive for killing Vivarini—or at least you can severally think up motives with which to confront one another. And in the case of each of you we now have a clue—a real, damning, mystery-story clue. There is a fairly simple explanation, is there not? One of you killed Vivarini, and deliberately planted two clues leading to the other two of you severally. If just one of these clues was noticed, there would be one suspect; if two, there would be an indication that two of you had been in collusion. But in addition to planting those two clues *deliberately*, the murderer also dropped one, pointing to himself, *inadvertently*. Would you agree'—and Appleby glanced from one to another of his companions—'that we now have an explanation of the observed facts?'

'A singularly rubbishing one,' Childrey said robustly.

'Very well, let me try again.' Appleby paused—and when he resumed speaking it was almost as if a current of icy air had begun to blow through the cottage. 'There *was* collusion, and between all three of you. And so incompetent have you been in your evil courses that you have all three made first-class errors. Childrey failed completely to destroy the papers he had managed to recover, and Gryde and Halberd both left physical traces of their presence in the lambing-hut. Will that do?'

'My dear Appleby, I fear you have a poor opinion of us.' Sweat was pouring down Gryde's face, but he managed to utter this with an air of mild mockery. 'Should we be *quite* so inept? And there's something you just haven't accounted for : you own damnably odd conduct.'

'Do you know, I'd call that right in the target area? Although I'd say it was not so much a matter of my conduct as of my mere presence.' With an air of conscious relaxation, Appleby began to fill his pipe. 'We were talking about co-incidence. Well, the really implausible coincidence was my being here at all. Don't you see? I was *meant* to be here. Vivarini wanted me here—and that although he and I were no more than casual acquaintances. That was the first thing in my head when I found him dead. And it led me straight to the truth.'

'The truth!' There was a dark flush on Halberd's face. 'You mean to say you know the *truth*, and you've been entertaining us to a lot of damned rubbish notwithstanding?'

'I certainly know the truth.'

'May we be favoured'—Gryde hissed this—'with some notion of when you arrived at it?'

'Oh, almost at once. Before I came in to tell you that Vivarini had been shot. First I *thought* for a few minutes, you know. It's always the advisable thing to do. And then I went to have a look at the gas cylinders. That settled it.'

'Vivarini,' Appleby said, 'didn't like any of you. You'd refused to publish him as a classic, you'd reviewed him waspishly, you'd been in a mess-up with him about a girl. But what he really resented was being treated as outmoded. His so-called Comedy of Discomfiture you all regarded as old hat. Well, he decided to treat you to a whiff of that Comedy all on your own.' Appleby paused. 'After all,' he said— blandly and with apparent inconsequence—'I was his guest, you know. I owed him something. It would have been a shame to knock that comedy too rapidly on the head.'

'The man was a devil,' Gryde said. 'And you're a devil too.'

'No, no—Vivarini wasn't really an evil man. He had me down so that there would be a sporting chance of giving you all no more than a bad half-hour.'

'Three hours.' Childrey had glanced at his watch.

'Very well. And I've no doubt that he'd taken other measures. A letter on its way to Australia, by surface mail, perhaps, and then due to come back the same way. At the worst you'd have had no more than a few months in quod.'

'Go on,' Halberd said grimly.

'There's very little to tell! He spread a few useful lies: that one of you had egged him on to arrange this fishing-party; that he was nurturing something between thoughts and intentions of suicide (although that was *not* a lie); that he had evidence of some discreditable sharp practice on Childrey's part. Then, similarly, he prepared his few useful clues: making that footprint, filching the cord from Gryde's dressing-gown, making his little imperfectly burnt heap of old business letters. After that, he had just one more thing to prepare.'

'You mean to tell us,' Halberd said, 'that he killed himself just for the fun of playing us a rotten trick?'

'Certainly. It was to be his last masterpiece in the Comedy of—'

'Yes, yes. But surely—'

'My dear Halberd, didn't you notice he was a sick man? It's my guess that he was very sick indeed—with no more than months, or perhaps weeks, before him.'

'My God—the poor devil! Ending his days with a revolting piece of malice.' Halberd frowned. 'What was that you said about gas cylinders?'

'There are three stored at the back of the cottage. Two contain butane, all right, but the third contains hydrogen. And all he needed apart from that was a fair-sized child's balloon—just not too big to go up that chimney. Plenty of lift in it to float away a very small gun. With this west wind, it must be over the North Sea by now. So you see why he had to die with his head in the fireplace—and why the doctor is puzzling over the odd position of the body.'

'The sergeant of police,' Gryde said, 'isn't puzzling over that footprint. Because you trampled it out of existence.'

There was a long silence while three exhausted fishermen stared at a retired Metropolitan Commissioner.

'It will be thought,' Appleby said, 'that Vivarini was shot by some professional criminal who had an eye on our wallets, and who knew he had major charges to face if he was apprehended. Something like that. The police don't always end up with an arrest, but they never fail to have a theory of the crime.'

'Is it going to be safe?' Gryde asked.

'Fairly safe, I'd suppose.' For the first time since his arrival at Dunwinnie, there was a hint of contempt in Appleby's voice. 'But safe or not, I judge it decent that this particular comedy of Frederick Vivarini's shall never be played before a larger audience than it has enjoyed tonight.'

THE CONVERSATION PIECE

LORD PENDRAGON WAS a British civil servant of
the old school. A King's Scholar at Eton, an Open Scholar
of Christ Church and for a leisured two years a Fellow of
New College, he had entered the Treasury and risen as far
as they rise—taking with him much literary cultivation,
artistic connoisseurship, musical taste and the like, in the
acquirement of which he had conceivably been assisted by
his substantial private fortune. As a young man Pendragon
had worked for Cabinet Ministers out of his own stable. He
used to exchange with them, when they lost their jobs,
suitable memorial trifles : perhaps a book bound for Jean
Grolier against one bound by Samuel Mearne. Later, he
worked with the same perfect discretion and good-humour
for New Men (as they were called at his club) whose private
interests, although perfectly reputable, were of a somewhat
different order. And now here he was, retired and silver-
haired, perhaps the most eminent guest at this small gathering at the Lyle Gallery, distinguished from his fellows only
by a slight excess of that air of perfect diffidence which
marks the English gentleman.

The Lyle is, of course, one of the major picture galleries
of the world, and this was why Lady Finch had chosen it to
receive her Conversation Piece. The gift was in memory of
her late husband, Sir Gabriel Finch, the eminent financier.
Sir Gabriel had clearly been the life and soul of the convivial
occasion depicted. The ladies had withdrawn; the male
guests were clustered round their host at the foot of his
dining-table; and the brilliant talk to which they were listening was agreeably symbolised or concretised in the crystal

83

and gold which the Finches abundantly commanded for the service of dessert. Word had gone round the small gathering at the Lyle that what was particularly to be admired was the *trompe-l'oeil* effect with which the artist had rendered the cherry-stones and walnut-shells on the silver-gilt plates. Some of the more self-assured of Lady Finch's friends were affecting to make this aesthetic discovery for themselves.

Of course there were levels of appreciation, each with its own vocabulary. The Director of the Lyle murmured to Judith Appleby that nobody would have expected the poor devil to turn himself into a *quadraturista*. The poor devil was the painter, Gwilym Lloyd. Lloyd—whom the uncharitable wit of the studios had nicknamed Mungo long before his death—had as a young man been regarded as the most promising painter of his generation. Then he had married, surrounded himself with a numerous progeny, and settled down as a ruthless manufacturer of boardroom portraits. Mungo Lloyd ended up as an R.A.—he, like Lord Pendragon, had risen as far as they rise—and it was possible that the Conversation Piece had been the turning-point in his career. So the picture had, for the informed, a certain sombre historical interest. Moreover, extremely few people had ever seen it before. It had hung in some private sanctum of the late Sir Gabriel's, accessible only to the regard of the particular cronies of its proprietor—who had presumably included the four persons here represented with him over their port and cigars. It was perhaps this fact that had brought the Applebys to have a look at the thing now.

'Do you find it amusing?' Lady Finch asked. Lady Finch, whether correctly or not, had taken on the role of hostess on this artistic occasion, and was having a word with everybody in turn.

'No, not exactly that.' Appleby judged the question odd. Apart from a formal introduction, Lady Finch was unknown to him, and he now glanced at her with attention. A harmless vacuous woman, she seemed to be. 'But extremely interesting. It captures a great deal of a certain style of living. You have very generously given the gallery what must become a notable period piece.'

'Do you think so?' These simple remarks seemed rather beyond Lady Finch. 'Gabriel always appeared to find it *very* amusing. And his friends. They had a gathering before it once a year. With champagne. And there was a great deal of laughter.'

'Dear me! And by his friends you mean, in this connection, the people actually represented with him here in the picture?'

'Yes. At least, I suppose so.' Lady Finch glanced vaguely at her handsome gift to the nation. 'I didn't really know my husband's business associates very well. Of course, they were important people. Everybody looked up to them—almost as much as to Gabriel himself.'

'I am delighted to hear it,' Appleby said. Lady Finch's first appearance before society, he was vaguely conjecturing, had perhaps been across the footlights of a music-hall. 'Did you know the artist, Gwilym Lloyd?'

'I only met him two or three times, during the sittings. They called him Mungo Lloyd, which was some sort of pun. But I thought him very astute. Gabriel did a great deal for him. After the Conversation Piece, I mean. Gabriel got him commissions for portraits all over the City. It was quite the making of Mr Lloyd. He became very good at robes and things. And fur. Aldermen and people have to be painted in fur.'

'Indeed they do. I think Lloyd died some years before Sir Gabriel. Was Sir Gabriel distressed?'

'Oh yes, of course. Gabriel's feelings were always the proper ones. Only, he used to *say* funny things. And I remember that when Mr Lloyd died he said it was a good riddance of a damned nuisance. Wasn't that strange?'

'Very,' Appleby said. And he made his escape with a bow.

*　　*　　*

It was into the arms of Lord Pendragon, whose dress and glass of tomato-juice alike suggested that he was going on to a formal dinner. He was, Appleby imagined, a Trustee of the Lyle, and present on this occasion as a matter of civility.

'Keeping an eye on security?' Pendragon asked humorously. It was the year in which Appleby had become Commissioner of Metropolitan Police, so here were two Top People in a huddle. 'Can't say I'd mind if somebody made off with the thing right under your nose, my dear fellow.'

'The Lloyd Conversation Piece? I quite agree—and I'm here merely because Judith brought me. By the way, who are the other people in the picture?'

'I haven't the slightest idea—and there seems to be nothing to inform us. Let's have another look at them.'

'They seem younger than their entertainer, and one might expect some of them to be still alive, and present to see themselves attaining fresh celebrity tonight. But Lady Finch is entirely vague about them.'

'A charming woman, but not notably well-informed.' With this bland pronouncement, Pendragon paused before the Conversation Piece. 'I knew Finch slightly,' he said, 'and it's a good likeness, so far as I remember. As for the others, I'm not sure now that they don't ring some vague bell. They hang together, as it were.' He frowned. 'But not much of a set, I'd say.'

Allowing for Lord Pendragon's professional caution, Appleby thought, this was a fairly stiff judgement on the late Sir Gabriel and his friends. 'I've just heard,' he offered experimentally, 'that they drank champagne in front of the thing once a year.'

'The devil they did! Some precious anniversary occasion, I don't doubt.' Pendragon's frown had deepened. And suddenly he made a surprising dive at the Conversation Piece, and pretty well rubbed noses with it. 'Well, I'm damned!' Lord Pendragon was so unwontedly loud in this exclamation that he attracted the attention of several people standing by. 'Must have one of Beckett's boffins look into this.'

Beckett was the name of the Lyle's Director, and at this moment he came up with Judith Appleby.

'Judith, my dear, you look ravishing,' Lord Pendragon said. 'And how is young Bobby getting on at Balliol? Do tell me.' It was against Pendragon's rules to expect a lady to pick up on a conversation in progress, and for some minutes he showed himself amiably conversant with Appleby family affairs. Then he glanced at his watch—with an openness that made the action entirely polite. 'Oh, great God!' he murmured. 'I have to dine with the Honourable Company of Comfiters—and no doubt talk to the chief comfit-maker's wife. Lucky I'm a shade more tolerant than Hotspur, eh?' And on this graceful Shakespearian note the retired Secretary of the Cabinet made his way to Lady Finch. The ensuing leave-taking had every appearance of the largest leisure. Its actual duration, Appleby remarked, was fifteen seconds.

When the Applebys got home at midnight—for they had gone to a theatre—there was a young man waiting in the hall. He was from 'C' Department, and this was the big moment of his career to date.

'Sir,' he said, 'the Commander thinks you should be let know at once. Lord Pendragon has been shot dead at a banquet in the City.'

Appleby—without, he hoped, treading on too many subordinate toes—investigated this curious affair himself. It appeared that, on arriving at Comfiters' Hall, Pendragon had entered a cloakroom, and from there a wash-place which happened to be deserted for the moment. He had been followed by his assailant wholly unobserved, and killed while slipping the ribbon of some decoration or other over his head. The enamel of the august gewgaw—macabrely enough—had been chipped by the bullet as it emerged through his forehead. The murderer must then simply have walked out again. It was one of those crimes the complete simplicity of which detectives find daunting and ominous.

Pendragon was a bachelor. A younger brother, a Professor of Jurisprudence at Cambridge, was properly distressed. He was also extremely insistent that the affair should be cleared up at once. It is not good for an eminent person's posthumous reputation to be mysteriously murdered. Something shady is inclined to hint itself as in the background of so sensational a demise.

Appleby believed in speed, for he knew that one's best chance of closing in on a crime effectively lies within the twenty-four hours following its commission. Yet it was a couple of days before he came round to the notion (so bizarre did it seem) that Lady Finch's Conversation Piece might have a place in the picture.

'Listen,' he said to Judith. 'That damned daub of Mungo Lloyd's—do you remember how oddly Pendragon behaved before it?'

'Oddly?'

'He took what you might call a lunge at it. I believe he suddenly recognised one of those four men depicted along with Finch, and found something startling in the fact. Indeed, he pretty well cried aloud about it. And I suspect his doing so alerted somebody to danger.'

'It wasn't that sort of lunge.'

'Just what do you mean by that, please?' Appleby was all attention at once. His wife was by profession a sculptor, and her perceptions before any work of art were likely to be acute.

'Pendragon wasn't looking at a face. He wasn't looking at anything that could be called representational at all—not like all those idiotic women at the cherry-stones and the drops of wine on the empty glasses. He was looking at something in the *facture*. Or the *fattura*, as our Italianate friend Beckett would say. And as I came up I heard him *say* something about Beckett. What was it?'

'That one of Beckett's boffins must look into the thing.'

'Good. And with infra-red light, if you ask me. The *fattura*, you know, is what I'd call the handling.' Judith paused. 'So *now* do you see?' she asked modestly.

Appleby wasted no time on a reply. He picked up the telephone, called for his car, and returned to the Lyle Gallery.

That afternoon a boffin did his stuff. Indeed, several boffins did their stuff. And the following day took Appleby into a world remote from such specialised delvers beneath the surface of things : into the world, indeed, of high finance. Sundry persons with long memories therein were induced to view the Conversation Piece. They left the Lyle looking grim.

On the third day—and after his brother's funeral—the Professor from Cambridge turned up again.

'Well,' he demanded of Appleby, 'is somebody going to hang for it?'

'My dear sir, I need hardly remind a lawyer that in England—'

'Yes, of course. Say, brought to book.'

'Frankly, the point is problematical. Everything is clear enough. But its oddity may trouble a jury—particularly as we shall have only circumstantial evidence to offer about who fired that shot.'

'Explain, please.'

'Certainly. And, first, I believe your brother did more or less tumble to the identity of the people in the picture—or to that of all but one of them—and had some notion of its audacious significance. But, for the moment, he kept mum.'

'He'd had a long training in discretion.'

'Precisely. And now, let's go back a bit. You recall the *Peseta* Affair?'

'Lord, yes. Chaps dealing dubiously in foreign currencies, and some suspicion that they'd obtained information from a confidential source for a corrupt consideration.'

'Just that. And they had an uncommonly close shave: Finch himself, and three associates called Hammond, Hartley, and Henderson.'

'Respectable if colourless names.'

'No doubt. And you can see all of them in the Conversation Piece. They've been identified for me half-a-dozen times over.'

'Did Finch's wife—'

'She hasn't a clue, and never had. Her husband's affairs were a sealed book to her. Now, about these men. Finch is dead and so is Hartley. Hammond and Henderson are alive. And Henderson, although apparently not invited, was at our curious occasion at the Lyle. I'm afraid it's the most awkward fact we have about him—so far.'

'You have left one man in the picture unaccounted for.'

'Yes, indeed. We'll call him, for the moment, the Fifth Man. Nobody I've been able to bring along has identified *him*.'

'I see.' The Professor considered. 'If that Conversation Piece represents the outrageous act of impudence I think it does, then we know at least something about the Fifth Man. He was in on that unscrupulous and successful financial *coup*.'

'Obviously. For the painter they call Mungo Lloyd—now dead—was brought in simply to celebrate and commemorate those people's triumphant dishonesty. No wonder they drank champagne before it every year.'

'Good God, Appleby—what a crowd!'

'Ah, yes—but now consider. The Conversation Piece was vainglorious—but in some way it must have been *rash* as well.'

'Rash?'

'Very rash—to have produced the eventual catastrophe it *has* produced. And there's the curious fact that, right up to his death, Gwilym Lloyd had some sort of hold over Finch. He obliged Finch to get him no end of profitable commissions around the City. And when Lloyd died Finch went on record —through his guileless wife—as saying that it was a good riddance of a damned nuisance. What do you make of that?'

'Not much.' The Professor smiled slowly. 'Although it leads my mind back to the Fifth Man.'

'As well it may. And one can think of an obvious reason why he has escaped identification so far. He belongs right outside the group, or clique, or gang—or whatever you care to call it. In fact, he's the confidential source from whom the vital financial information came—or was bought, as we may safely suppose.'

'Was any individual actually suspected at the time?'

'Yes. Antony Hopcroft was.'

There was a long silence in Sir John Appleby's study. The only sound was the soft clink of ice setting in a glass, since Appleby had provided the Professor with the sort of recruitment which the aftermath of a funeral commonly requires.

'Good God!' The Professor barely whispered this. 'Antony was one of my brother's closest colleagues—and impeccable.'

'So one would have supposed. Yet a certain amount of evidence wasn't lacking. Where any hope of an effective prosecution broke down, however, was in the fact that not the slightest trace of any connection between Finch's group and Hopcroft could be found.'

'And yet you suggest that here he was in this foolhardy picture?' The Professor had suddenly transfixed Appleby with a scholar's cold intellectual stare. 'It would certainly be in the picture in another sense—the psychological picture, so to speak—of those arrogant champagne-swilling rascals. But it won't do. My brother would have recognised Hopcroft's portrait at once.' The Professor's gaze hardened further. 'Do you suggest that he did, and that he concealed the fact from you?'

'Nothing of the kind. What your brother did spot in the

picture, he spotted because he was something of a connoisseur. The Fifth Man's head is a piece of over-painting, and is by a hand other than Lloyd's. The supreme impudence of the picture as it originally was consisted in its depicting Antony Hopcroft as a member of the group. Lloyd must have understood the significance of this, or he wouldn't have had that hold over Finch. Later on—and it was after Lloyd's death—Finch decided the joke was too risky to perpetuate. He could, of course, simply have destroyed the Conversation Piece, but that might have caused awkward questions to be asked. So he had in another painter, and Hopcroft's head disappeared beneath an imaginary head—that of our Fifth Man.'

'And this fellow Henderson—the Fourth Man, as we may say?'

'As I've told you, Henderson was present at the party in the Lyle. When he saw your brother spot the faking, and overheard him throw out that suggestion about a boffin, he saw instantly that the whole *Peseta* Affair might bob up again, this new piece of evidence be adduced, and a successful criminal prosecution achieved. But Beckett, the Director, hadn't heard the boffin bit, and your brother had at once left the party. Silence him, and nobody would ever have a second thought about the Conversation Piece again.'

'Do you mean to say—'

'Excuse me.' Appleby's telephone had rung, and he picked up the instrument. 'Thank you,' he said unemotionally a minute later, and put it down again. 'A development, Professor. Henderson was identified slipping out of the Comfiters' premises, after all. By a commissionaire who had worked for one of his companies.' Appleby glanced at a calendar. 'Friday wasn't Henderson's lucky day.'

'Nor was it my brother's,' the Professor said sadly.

DEATH BY WATER

SIR JOHN APPLEBY had been worried about
Charles Vandervell for some time. But this was probably
true of a good many of the philosopher's friends. Vandervell's
speculations, one of these had wittily remarked, could be
conceived as going well or ill according to the sense one was
prepared to accord that term. His last book, entitled
(mysteriously to the uninstructed) *Social Life as a Sign
System*, had been respectfully received by those who went
in for that kind of thing; but it was clear that something
had gone badly wrong with his investments. He was what is
called a private scholar, for long unattached to any university
or other salary-yielding institution, and had for years lived
very comfortably indeed on inherited wealth of an unspecified
but doubtless wholly respectable sort.

He was not a landed man. His country house, pleasantly
situated a few miles from the Cornish coast, owned extensive
gardens but was unsupported by any surrounding agricultural
activities. The dividends came in, and that was that. Nobody
could have thought of it as a particularly vulnerable condition. Some adverse change in the state of the national
economy might be expected from time to time to produce a
correspondingly adverse effect upon an income such as his.
But it would surely require recessions, depressions and slumps
of a major order to result in anything like catastrophe.

Vandervell himself was vague about the whole thing.
This might have been put down to simple incompetence,
since it would certainly have been difficult to imagine a man
with less of a head for practical affairs. But there were those
who maintained that some feeling of guilt was operative as

well. Vandervell was uneasy about living a life of leisure on the labours of others, and was unwilling to face up to considering his mundane affairs at all. He occasionally spoke in an old-fashioned way about his 'man of business'. Nobody had ever met this personage, or could so much as name him; but it was obvious that he must occupy a key position in the conduct of his client's monetary affairs. Vandervell himself acknowledged this. 'Bound to say,' he had once declared to Appleby, 'that my financial wizard earns his fees. No hope of keeping my chin above water at all, if I didn't have him on the job. And even as it is, I can't be said to be doing too well.'

For some months this last persuasion had been gaining on Vandervell rapidly and throwing him into ever deepening gloom. One reading of this was clearly that the gloom was pathological and irrational—a depressive state generated entirely within the unfortunate man's own head—and that a mere fantasy of being hard up, quite unrelated to the objective facts of the case, was one distressing symptom of his condition. One does hear every now and then, after all, of quite wealthy people who have stopped the milk and the newspaper out of a firm conviction they can no longer pay for them. There was a point at which Appleby took this view of Vandervell's state of mind. Vandervell was a fairly prolific writer, and his essays and papers began to suggest that the adverse state of his bank balance (whether real or imagined) was bringing him to a vision of the universe at large as weighted against him and all mankind in an equally disagreeable way. Hitherto his philosophical work had been of a severely intellectual and dispassionate order. Now he produced in rapid succession a paper on Schopenhauer, a paper on von Hartmann, and a long essay called *Existentialism and the Metaphysic of Despair*. All this didn't precisely suggest cheerfulness breaking in.

This was the state of the case when Appleby encountered

Vandervell's nephew, Fabian Vandervell, in a picture gallery off Bond Street and took him to his club for lunch.

'How is your uncle getting along?' Appleby asked. 'He doesn't seem to come much to town nowadays, and it's a long time since I've been down your way.'

Fabian, who was a painter, also lived in Cornwall—more or less in a colony of artists in a small fishing village called Targan Bay. As his uncle was a bachelor, and he himself his only near relation, it was generally assumed that he would prove to be his uncle's heir. The prospect was probably important to him, since nobody had ever heard of Fabian's selling a picture. So Fabian too might well be concerned at the manner in which the family fortunes were said to be in a decline.

'He muddles along,' Fabian said. 'And his interests continue to change for the worse, if you ask me. Did you ever hear of a book called *Biathanatos*?'

'It rings a faint bell.'

'It's by John Donne, and is all about what Donne liked to call "the scandalous disease of headlong dying". It caused a bit of a scandal, I imagine. Donne was Dean of St Paul's, you remember, as well as a poet; so he had no business to be fudging up an apology for suicide. Uncle Charles is talking about editing *Biathanatos*, complete with his own learned commentary on the theme. Morbid notion.' Fabian paused. 'Uncommonly nice claret you have here.'

'I'm delighted you approve of it.' Appleby noticed that the modest decanter of the wine with which Fabian had been provided was already empty. 'Do you mean that you are alarmed about your uncle?'

'Well, he does talk about suicide in a general way, as well. But perhaps there's no great cause for alarm.'

'We'll hope not.' Appleby decided not to pursue this topic, which it didn't strike him as his business to discuss. 'I have it in mind to call in on your uncle, incidentally, in a few weeks' time, when I go down to visit my sister at Bude. And now I want you to explain to me those pictures we both found ourselves looking at this morning. Puzzling things to one of my generation.'

Fabian Vandervell proved perfectly willing to accept this invitation. He held forth contentedly for the rest of the meal.

Appleby fulfilled his intention a month later, and his first impression was that Charles Vandervell had become rather a lonely man. Pentallon Hall was a substantial dwelling, yet apart from its owner only an elderly manservant called Litter was much in evidence. But at least one gardener must be lurking around, since the extensive grounds which shielded the place from the general surrounding bleakness of the Cornish scene were all in apple-pie order. Vandervell led Appleby over all this with the air of a country gentleman who has nothing in his head except the small concerns which the managing of such a property must generate. But the role wasn't quite native to the man; and in an indefinable way none of the interests or projects which he paraded appeared quite to be coming off. Vandervell had a theory about bees, but the Pentallon bees were refusing to back it up. In a series of somewhat suburban-looking ponds he bred tropical fish, but even the mild Cornish climate didn't suit these creatures at all. Nor at the moment did it suit the roses Vandervell was proposing to exhibit at some local flower show later in the season; they were plainly (like so much human hope and aspiration, their owner commented morosely) nipped in the bud. All in all, Charles Vandervell was revealing himself more than ever as a man not booked for much success except, conceivably, within certain rather specialised kingdoms of the mind.

Or so Appleby thought until Mrs Mountmorris arrived. Mrs Mountmorris was apparently a near neighbour and almost certainly a widow; and Mrs Mountmorris came to tea. Litter took her arrival distinguishably in ill part; he was a privileged retainer of long standing, and seemingly licenced to express himself in such matters through the instrumentality of heavy sighs and sour looks. Vandervell, on the other hand, brightened up so markedly when the lady was announced that Appleby at once concluded Litter to have rational ground for viewing her as a threat to the established order of things at Pentallon. Moreover Vandervell took considerable pleasure in presenting Appleby to the new arrival, and Mrs Mountmorris obligingly played up by treating her host's friend as a celebrity. It was, of course, a quiet part of the world. But Appleby, being well aware of Vandervell as owning a distinction of quite another flight to any attainable by a policeman, found in this piece of nonsense something a little touching as well as absurd.

Not that, beneath an instant social competence, Mrs Mountmorris was in the least pleased at finding another visitor around. She marked herself at once as a woman of strong character, and perhaps as one who was making it her business to take her philosophic neighbour in hand. If that was it—if she had decided to organise Charles Vandervell—then organised Charles Vandervell would be. On the man's chances of escape, Appleby told himself, he wouldn't wager so much as a bottle of that respectable claret to which he had entertained Vandervell's nephew Fabian at his club. And Fabian, if he knew about the lady, would certainly take as dark a view of her as Litter did.

'Charles's roses,' Mrs Mountmorris said, 'refuse to bloom. His bees produce honey no different from yours, Sir John, or mine.' Mrs Mountmorris paused to dispense tea—a duty which, to Litter's visible displeasure, she had made no bones about taking to herself. 'As for his ships, they just won't come home. *Mais nous changerons tout cela.*'

This, whatever one thought of the French, was nothing if not forthright, and Appleby glanced at the lady with some respect.

'But a philosopher's argosies,' he said a shade pedantically, 'must voyage in distant waters, don't you think? They may return all the more richly freighted in the end.'

'Of *that* I have no doubt.' Mrs Mountmorris spoke briskly and dismissively, although the dismissiveness may have been directed primarily at Appleby's flight of fancy. 'But practical issues have to be considered as well. And Charles, I think, has come to agree with me. Charles?'

'Yes, of course.' Thus abruptly challenged, Vandervell would have had to be described as mumbling his reply. At the same time, however, he was gazing at his female friend in an admiration there was no mistaking.

'Has that man turned up yet?' Mrs Mountmorris handed Vandervell his tea-cup, and at the same time indicated that he might consume a cucumber sandwich. 'The show-down is overdue.'

'Yes, of course.' Vandervell reiterated with a nervous nod what appeared to be his *leit-motif* in Mrs Mountmorris's presence. 'And I've sent for him. An absolute summons, I assure you. And you and I must have a talk about it, *tête-à-tête*, soon.'

'Indeed we must.' Mrs Mountmorris was too well-bred not to accept this as closing the mysterious topic she had introduced. 'And as for *these*'—and she gestured at an unpromising rose-bed in the near vicinity of which the tea-table was disposed—'derris dust is the answer, and nothing else.'

After this, Appleby didn't linger at Pentallon for very long. His own call had been casual and unheralded. It would be tactful to let that *tête-à-tête* take place sooner rather than later. Driving on to his sister's house at Bude, he reflected that Mrs Mountmorris must be categorised as a good thing. Signs were not wanting that she was putting stuffing into Charles Vandervell, of late so inclined to unwholesome meditation on headlong dying. It was almost as if a worm were going to turn. Yet one ought not, perhaps, to jump to conclusions. On an off-day, and to a diffident and resigned man, the lady might well assume the character of a last straw herself. Litter, certainly, was already seeing her in that light. His gloom as he politely performed the onerous duty of opening the door of Appleby's car, suggested his being in no doubt, at least, that the roses would be deluged in derris dust before the day was out.

Appleby hadn't, however, left Pentallon without a promise to call in on his return journey, which took place a week later. This time, he rang up to announce his arrival. He didn't again want to find himself that sort of awkward extra whom the Italians style a *terzo incomodo*.

Litter answered the telephone, and in a manner which instantly communicated considerable agitation. Mr Vandervell, he said abruptly, was not in residence. Then, as if recalling his training, he desired Appleby to repeat his name, that he might apprise his employer of the inquiry on his return.

'Sir John Appleby.'

'Oh, yes, sir—yes, indeed.' It was as if a penny had dropped in the butler's sombre mind. 'Pray let me detain you for a moment, Sir John. We are in some distress at Pentallon—really very perturbed, sir. The fact is that Mr Vandervell has disappeared. Without a trace, Sir John, as the newspapers sometimes express it. Except that I have received a letter from him—a letter susceptible of the most shocking interpretation.' Litter paused on this—as if it were a phrase in which, even amid the perturbation to which he had referred, he took a certain just satisfaction. 'To tell you the truth, sir, I have felt it my duty to inform the police. I wonder whether you could possibly break your journey here, as you had proposed? I know your reputation, Sir John, begging your pardon.'

'My dear Litter, my reputation scarcely entitles me to impose myself on the Cornish constabulary. Are they with you now?'

'Not just at the moment, sir. They come and go, you might

say. And very civil they are. But it's not at all the kind of thing we are accustomed to.'

'I suppose not. Is there anybody else at Pentallon?'

'Mr Fabian has arrived from Targan Bay. And Mr Truebody, sir, who is understood to look after Mr Vandervell's affairs.'

'It's Mr Truebody whom Mr Vandervell refers to as his man of business?'

'Just so, sir. I wonder whether you would care to speak to Mr Fabian? He is in the library now, sorting through his uncle's papers.'

'The devil he is.' Appleby's professional instinct was alerted by this scrap of information. 'It mightn't be a bad idea. Be so good as to tell him I'm on the telephone.'

Within a minute of this, Fabian Vandervell's urgent voice was on the line.

'Appleby—is it really you? For God's sake come over to this accursed place quick. You must have gathered even from that moronic Litter that something pretty grim has happened to my uncle. Unless he's merely up to some ghastly foolery, the brute fact is that *Biathanatos* has nobbled him. You're a family friend—'

'I'm on the way,' Appleby said, and put down the receiver.

But Appleby's first call was at a police station, since there was a certain measure of protocol to observe. An hour later, and accompanied by a Detective Inspector called Gamley, he was in Charles Vandervell's library, and reading Charles Vandervell's letter.

My dear Litter,

There are parties one does not quit without making a round of the room, and just such a party I am now preparing to take my leave of. In this instance it must be a round of letters that is in question, and of these the first must assuredly be addressed to you, who have been so faithful a servant and friend. I need not particularise the manner of what I propose to do. This will reveal itself at a convenient time and prove, I hope, not to have been too untidy. And now, all my thanks! I am only sorry that the small token of my esteem which is to come to you must, in point of its amount, reflect the sadly embarrassed state of my affairs.

Yours sincerely,
CHARLES VANDERVELL

'Most affecting,' Mr Truebody said. 'Litter, I am sure you were very much moved.' Truebody was a large and powerful looking man, disadvantageously possessed of the sort of wildly staring eyes popularly associated with atrocious criminals. Perhaps it was to compensate for this that he exhibited a notably mild manner.

'It was upsetting, of course.' Litter said this in a wooden way. Since he had so evident a difficulty in liking anybody, it wasn't surprising that he didn't greatly care for the man of business. 'But we must all remember,' he added with mournful piety, 'that while there is life there is hope. A very sound proverb that is—if an opinion may be permitted me.'

'Exactly!' Fabian Vandervell, who had been standing in a window and staring out over the gardens, turned round and broke in unexpectedly. 'At first, I was quite bowled over by this thing. But I've been thinking. And it seems to me—'

'One thing at a time, Fabian.' Appleby handed the letter back to Gamley, who was in charge of it. 'Was this simply left on Mr Vandervell's desk, or something of that kind?'

'It came by post.'

'Then where's the envelope?'

'Mr Litter'—Gamley favoured the butler with rather a grim look—'has unfortunately failed to preserve it.'

'A matter of habit, sir.' Litter was suddenly extremely nervous. 'When I open a postal communication I commonly drop the outer cover straight into the waste-paper basket in my pantry. It was what I did on this occasion, and unfortunately the basket was emptied into an incinerator almost at once.'

'Did you notice the postmark?'

'I'm afraid not, sir.'

'The envelope, like the letter itself, was undoubtedly in Mr Vandervell's handwriting?'

'No, sir. The address was typewritten.'

'That's another point—and an uncommonly odd one.' Fabian had advanced to the centre of the room. 'It makes me feel the whole thing is merely funny-business, after all. And there's the further fact that the letter isn't dated. I'm inclined to think my uncle may simply have grabbed it from the pile, gone off Lord knows where, and then typed out an envelope and posted the thing in pursuance of some mere whim or fantasy.'

'Isn't that pretty well to declare him insane?' Appleby looked hard at Fabian. 'And just what do you mean by talking about a pile?'

'I believe he was always writing these things. Elegant valedictions. Making sure that nothing so became him in his life as—'

'We've had Donne; we needn't have Shakespeare too.' Appleby was impatient. 'I must say I don't find the notion of your uncle occasionally concocting such things in the least implausible, psychologically regarded. But is there any hard evidence?'

'I've been hunting around, as a matter of fact. In his papers, I mean. I can't say I've found anything. Uncle Charles may have destroyed any efforts of the kind when he cleared out, taking this prize specimen to Litter with him.'

'Isn't all this rather on the elaborate side?' Truebody asked, with much gentleness of manner. 'I am really afraid that we are failing to face the sad simplicity of the thing. Everybody acquainted with him knows that Vandervell has been turning increasingly melancholic. We just have to admit that this had reached a point at which he decided to make away with himself. So he wrote this perfectly genuine letter to Litter, and perhaps others we haven't yet heard of—'

'Why did he take it away and post it?' Inspector Gamley demanded.

'That's obvious enough, I should have thought. He wanted to avoid an immediate hue and cry, such as might have been started at once, had he simply left the letter to Litter behind him.'

'It's certainly a possibility,' Appleby said. 'Would you consider, Mr Truebody, that such a delaying tactic on Vandervell's part may afford some clue to the precise way in which he intended to commit suicide? He tells Litter it isn't going to be too untidy.'

'I fear I am without an answer, Sir John. The common thing, where a country gentleman is in question, is to take out a shot-gun and fake a more or less plausible accident at a stile. But Vandervell clearly didn't propose any faking. The letter-writing shows that his suicide was to be declared and open. I feel that this goes with his deepening morbidity.'

'But that's not, if you ask me, how Mr Vandervell was feeling at all.' Litter had spoken suddenly and with surprising energy. 'For he'd taken the turn, as they say. Or that's my opinion.'

'And just what might you mean by that, Mr Litter?' Gamley had produced a notebook, as if he felt in the presence of too much unrecorded chat.

'I mean that what Mr Truebody says isn't what you might call up to date. More than once, just lately, I've told myself Mr Vandervell was cheering up a trifle—and high time, too. More confident, in a manner of speaking. Told me off once or twice about this or that. I can't say I was pleased at the time. But it's what makes me a little hopeful now.'

'This more aggressive stance on your employer's part,' Appleby asked, 'disposes you against the view that he must indeed have committed suicide?'

'Yes, Sir John. Just that.'

There was a short silence, which was broken by a constable's entering the library. He walked up to Gamley, and then hesitated—as if doubtful whether what he had to say ought to be communicated to the company at large. Then he took the plunge.

'Definite news at last, sir. And just what we've been afraid of. They've discovered Mr Vandervell's body—washed up on a beach near Targan Bay.'

'Drowned, you mean?'

'Yes, sir. Beyond doubt, the report says. And they're looking for his clothes now.'

'His clothes?'

'Just that, sir. The body was stark naked.'

Although the North Cornish coast was only a few miles away, Charles Vandervell owned no regular habit of bathing there—this even although he was known to be an accomplished swimmer. Even if the letter to Litter had never been written, it would have had to be judged extremely improbable that his death could be accounted for as an accident following upon a sudden whim to go bathing. For one thing, Targan Bay and its environs, although little built over, were not so unfrequented that a man of conventional instincts (and Vandervell was that) would have been likely to dispense with some decent scrap of swimming apparel. On the other hand—or this, at least, was the opinion expressed by his nephew—a resolution to drown himself might well have been accompanied by just that. To strip naked and swim straight out to sea could well have come to him as the tidy thing.

Yet there were other possibilities, and Appleby saw one of them at once. The sea—and particularly a Cornish sea—can perform astonishing tricks with a drowned man. It can transform into a nude corpse a sailor who has gone overboard in oilskins, sea-boots, and a great deal else. It can thus cast up a body itself unblemished. Or it can go on to whip and lacerate such a body to a grim effect of sadistic frenzy. Or it can set its own living creatures, tiny perhaps but multitudinous, nibbling and worrying till the bones appear. What particular fate awaits a body is all a matter of rocks and shoals—shoals in either sense—and of currents and tides.

Appleby had a feeling that the sea might yield up some further secret about Charles Vandervell yet. Meantime, it was to be hoped there was more to be learnt on land. The circumstances of the missing man's disappearance plainly needed investigation.

Appleby's first visit to Pentallon had been on a Monday, and it was a Monday again now. According to Litter, the remainder of that first Monday had been uneventful, except in two minor regards. The formidable Mrs Mountmorris had stayed on almost till dinner-time, which wasn't Litter's notion of an afternoon call. There had been a business discussion of some sort, and it had been conducted with sufficient circumspection to prevent Litter, who had been curious, from hearing so many as half a dozen illuminating words. But Litter rather supposed (since one must speak frankly in face of a crisis like the present) that the lady had more than a thought of abandoning her widowed state, and that she was in process of thoroughly sorting out Vandervell's affairs before committing herself. When she had at length gone away Vandervell had made a number of telephone calls. At dinner he had been quite cheerful—or perhaps it would be better to say that he had appeared to be in a state of rather grim satisfaction. Litter confessed to having been a little uncertain of his employer's wave-length.

On the Tuesday morning Mr Truebody had turned up at Pentallon, but hadn't stayed long. Litter had received the impression—just in passing the library door, as he had several times been obliged to do—that Mr Truebody was receiving instructions or requests which were being pretty forcefully expressed. No doubt Mr Truebody himself would speak as to that. There had been no question, Litter opined, of the two gentlemen having words. Or it might be better to say there had been no question of their having a row—not as there had been with Mr Fabian when he turned up on the same afternoon. And about *that*—Litter supposed—Mr Fabian would speak.

This sensational disclosure on Litter's part could have been aimed only at Appleby, since Inspector Gamley turned out to have been treated to it already. And Fabian seemed to have made no secret of what he now termed lightly a bit of a tiff. He had formed the same conjecture about Mrs Mount-morris's intentions as Litter had done, and he was ready to acknowledge that the matter wasn't his business. But between him and his uncle there was some obscure matter of a small family trust. In the changed situation now showing every sign of blowing up he had come to Pentallon resolved to get this clarified. His uncle had been, in his view, quite unjustifiably short with him, saying that he had much more important things on his mind. So a bit of a rumpus there had undoubtedly been. But as he had neither carried Uncle Charles out to sea and drowned him, nor so effectively bullied him as to make him go and drown himself, he really failed to see that Litter's coming up with the matter had much point.

Listening to all this, Appleby was not wholly indisposed to agree. He had a long experience of major catastrophes bringing unedifying episodes of a minor order to light. So he went on to inquire about the Wednesday, which looked as if it might have been the point of crisis.

And Wednesday displayed what Inspector Gamley called a pattern. It was the day of the week upon which Pentallon's two maidservants, who were sisters, enjoyed their free half-day together. Immediately after lunch, Vandervell had started fussing about the non-delivery of a consignment of wine from his merchant in Bristol. He had shown no particular interest about this negligence before, but now he had ordered Litter to get into a car and fetch the stuff from Bristol forthwith. And as soon as Litter had departed in some indignation on this errand (Bristol being, as he pointed out, a hundred miles away, if it was a step) Vandervell had accorded both his gardener and his gardener's boy the same treatment—the quest, this time, being directed to Exeter and a variety of horticultural needs (derris dust among them, no doubt). Apart from its proprietor, Pentallon was thus dis-populated until the late evening. When Litter himself re-turned it was in a very bad temper, so that he retired to his own quarters for the night without any attempt to report himself to his employer. And as his first daily duty in the way of personal attendance was to serve lunch, and as the maids (as he explained) were both uncommonly stupid girls, it was not until after midday on Thursday that there was a general recognition of something being amiss. And at this point Litter had taken it into his head that he must behave with discretion, and not precipitately spread abroad the fact of what might be no more than eccentric (and perhaps obscurely improper) behaviour on the part of the master of Pentallon.

The consequence of all this was that it took Charles Vandervell's letter, delivered on the Friday, to stir Litter into alerting the police. And by then Vandervell had been dead for some time. Even upon superficial examination, it appeared, the police surgeons were convinced of that.

Establishing this rough chronology satisfied Appleby for the moment, and he reminded himself that he was at Pentallon not as a remorseless investigator but merely as a friend of the dead man and his nephew. That Charles Vandervell *was* now definitely known to be dead no doubt meant for Inspector Gamley a switching to some new routine which he had better be left for a time to pursue undisturbed. So Appleby excused himself, left the house, and wandered thoughtfully through the gardens. The roses were still not doing too well, but what was on view had its interest, all the same. From a raised terrace walk remote from the house, moreover, there was a glimpse of the sea. Appleby had surveyed this for some moments when he became aware that he was no longer alone. Truebody, that somewhat mysterious man of business, had come up behind him.

'Are you quite satisfied with this picture, Sir John?' Truebody asked.

'This picture?' For a second Appleby supposed that here was an odd manner of referring to the view. Then he understood. 'I'd have to be clearer as to just what the picture is supposed to be before I could answer that one.'

'Why should Vandervell clear the decks—take care to get rid of Litter and the rest of them—if he was simply proposing to walk over *there*'—Truebody gestured towards the horizon—'for the purpose of drowning himself? The unnecessariness of the measure worries me. He could simply have said he was going for a normal sort of walk—or even that he was going out to dinner. He could have said half a dozen things. Don't you agree?'

'Yes, I think I do—in a way. But one has to allow for the fact that the mind of a man contemplating suicide is quite likely to work a shade oddly. Vandervell may simply have felt the need of a period of solitude, here at Pentallon, in which to arrive at a final decision about himself. Anyway, he *has* been drowned.'

'Indeed, yes. And his posting that letter immediately beforehand does seem to rule out accident. Unless, of course, he was putting on a turn.'

'A turn, Mr Truebody?'

'One of those just-short-of-suicide efforts which psychologists nowadays interpret as a cry for help.'

'That's often a valid enough explanation of unsuccessful suicide, no doubt. But what would the cry for help be designed to save him from? Would it be the embrace of that predatory Mrs Mountmorris?'

'It hadn't occurred to me that way.' Truebody looked

startled. 'But something else has. Say that Vandervell was expecting a visitor here at Pentallon, and that for some reason he didn't want the circumstance to be known. That would account for his clearing everybody out. Then the visit took place, and was somehow disastrous. Or perhaps it just *didn't* take place, and there was for some reason disaster in the mere fact of that. And it was only *then* that he decided to write that letter to Litter as a preliminary to walking down to the sea and drowning himself.' Truebody glanced sharply at Appleby. 'What do you think of that?'

'I think I'd call it the change-of-plan theory of Charles Vandervell's death. I don't know that I'd go all the way with it. But I have a sense of its being in the target area, of there having been some element of improvisation somehow in the affair. . . . Ah! Here is our friend the constable again.'

'Inspector Gamley's compliments, sir.' The constable appeared to feel that Appleby rated for considerable formality of address. 'A further message has just come through. They've found the dead man's clothes.'

'Abandoned somewhere on the shore?'

'Not exactly, sir. Washed up like the body itself, it seems —but in a small cove more than a mile farther west. That's our currents, sir. The Inspector has gone over to Targan Bay at once. He wonders if you'd care to follow him.'

'Thank you. I'll drive over now.'

Vandervell's body had been removed for immediate post-mortem examination, so it was only his clothes that were on view. And of these most were missing. It was merely a jacket and trousers, entangled in each other and grotesquely entwined in seaweed, that had come ashore. Everything else was probably lost for good.

'Would he have gone out in a boat?' Appleby asked.

'I'd hardly think so.' Gamley shook his head. 'One way up or the other, such a craft would have been found by now. I'd say he left his clothes close to the water, and they were taken out by the tide. Now they're back again. Not much doubt they've been in the sea for about as long as Vandervell himself was.'

'Anything in the pockets—wallet, watch, that kind of thing?'

'Both these, and nothing else.' Gamley smiled grimly. 'Except for what you might call one or two visitors. All laid out next door. Would you care to see?'

'Decidedly so, Inspector. But what do you mean by visitors?'

'Oh, just these.' Gamley had ushered Appleby into the next room in the Targan Bay police station, and was pointing at a table. 'Inquisitive creatures, one gets in these waters. The crab was up a trouser-leg, and the little fish snug in the breast-pocket of the jacket.'

'I see.' Appleby peered at these odd exhibits. 'I see,' he repeated, but on a different note. 'Will that post-mortem have begun?'

'Almost sure to have.'

'Then get on to them at once. Tell them—very, very tactfully—to be particularly careful about the bottom of the lungs. Then I'll put through a call to London myself, Inspector. We must have a top ichthyologist down by the night train.'

'A *what*, sir?'

'Authority on fish, Inspector. And there's another thing. You can't risk an arrest quite yet. But you can make damned sure somebody doesn't get away.'

Appleby offered explanations on the following afternoon.

'It has been my experience that the cleverest criminals are often prone to doing some one, isolated stupid thing— particularly when under pressure, and driven to improvise. In this case it lay in the decision to post that letter to Litter, instead of just leaving it around. The idea was to achieve a delaying tactic, and there was a sense in which a typewritten address would be safer than one which forged Vandervell's hand. But it introduced at once what was at least a small implausibility. Vandervell while obsessed with suicide may well have prepared a dozen such letters, and without getting round to either addressing or dating them. But if he later decided that one of them was really to be delivered—and delivered through the post—the natural thing would simply be to pick up an envelope and address it by hand.'

'Was that the chap's only bad slip-up?'

'Not exactly. The crime must be called one of calculation and premeditation, I suppose, since the idea was to get the perpetrator out of a tough spot. But its actual commission was rash and unthinking, so that it left him in a tougher spot still. Consider, for a start, the several steps that led to it. Charles Vandervell's supposed financial reverses and stringencies were entirely a consequence of sustained and ingenious speculations on Truebody's part. They didn't, as a matter of fact, *need* to be all that ingenious, since our eminent philosopher's practical sense of such matters was about zero. But then Mrs Mountmorris enters the story. She is a very different proposition. Truebody is suddenly in extreme danger, and knows it. His client's attitude stiffens; in fact you may say the worm turns. Truebody is summoned to Pentallon, and appears on Tuesday morning. He is given only until the next day to show, if he can, that everything has been fair and above board, after all. But Charles Vandervell has a certain instinct for privacy. If there is to be a row, he doesn't want it bruited abroad. When Truebody comes back on Wednesday afternoon there is nobody else around. And I suppose that puts ideas in his head.'

'So he waits his chance?' Fabian Vandervell asked.

'Not exactly that. Imagine the two of them, walking around the gardens. Your uncle is a new man; he has this dishonest rascal cornered, and is showing grim satisfaction in the fact. He says roundly that he'll have Truebody prosecuted and gaoled. And, at that, Truebody simply hits out at him. He's a powerful fellow; and, for the moment at least, your uncle is knocked unconscious. It has all happened beside one of those small ponds with the tropical fish. So it is *now* that Truebody sees—or thinks he sees—his chance. He will stage some sort of accident, he tells himself. In a moment he has shoved your uncle into the pool. And there he holds him down until he drowns. So far, so good—or bad. But the accident looks a damned unlikely one, all the same. And then he remembers something.'

'*Biathanatos*, and all that.'

'Precisely so—and something more. Truebody has had plenty of opportunity, during business visits to Pentallon, to poke about among your uncle's papers. He remembers that batch of elegant farewells by a Charles Vandervell about to depart this life by his own hand—'

'But nobody would drown himself in a shallow fish-pond. It simply couldn't be done.'

'Exactly so, Fabian. And as soon as Truebody had slipped into the empty house and secured that batch of letters, he heaved your uncle's body into his car, and drove hard for the sea. And there, let us just say, he further did his stuff.'

'And later posted that letter to Litter. After which he had nothing to do but lie low—and get busy, no doubt, covering up on the financial side.'

'He didn't quite lie low. Rashly again, he took the initiative in holding rather an odd conversation with me. He thought it clever himself to advance one or two considerations which were bound to be in my head anyway.'

'And now he's under lock and key.' Fabian Vandervell frowned. 'Good Lord! I'm forgetting I still haven't the faintest notion how you tumbled to it all.'

'That was the shubunkin.'

'What the devil is that?'

'Small tropical fish—decidedly not found in the sea off Cornwall. A shubunkin deftly made its way into your uncle's breast-pocket while Truebody was holding him prone in that pool.'

'Well I'm damned! But it doesn't sound much on which to secure a conviction for murder.'

'It's not quite all, Fabian. In your uncle's lungs there was still quite a bit of the water he drowned in. Full of minute freshwater-pond life.'

A QUESTION OF CONFIDENCE

Bᴏʙʙʏ Aᴘᴘʟᴇʙʏ (sᴜᴄᴄᴇssꜰᴜʟ scrum-half retired, and author of that notable anti-novel *The Lumber Room*) had been down from Oxford for a couple of years. But he went back from time to time, sometimes for the day and sometimes on a week-end basis. He had a number of clever friends there who were now busily engaged in digging in for life. They had become, that is to say, junior dons of one or another more or less probationary sort, and had thereby risen from the austerities of undergraduate living to the fleshpots and the thrice-driven beds of down associated with Senior Common Rooms and High Tables. They liked entertaining Bobby, to whom *The Lumber Room* rather than his athletic prowess lent, in their circle, a certain prestige. One of these youths was a historian called Brian Button.

Button sometimes came home with Bobby to Long Dream. Sir John Appleby (policeman retired) rather liked this acquaintance of his son's, and was very accustomed to address him as B.B.—this seemingly with some elderly facetious reference to the deceased art historian Bernard Berenson. Bobby's B.B. (unlike the real B.B.) came from Yorkshire, a region of which Bobby's father approved. So Appleby was quite pleased when, chancing to look up from his writing-table on a sunny Saturday morning, he saw Bobby's ancient Porsche stationary on the drive, with Bobby climbing out of the driver's seat and B.B. out of the other. But the young men were unprovided with suitcases, which was odd. The young men bolted for the front door as if through a thunderstorm, which was odder still. And seconds later—what was oddest of all—the young men burst without ceremony into the room.

'Daddy!' the distinguished novelist exclaimed—and he seemed positively out of breath—'here's an awful thing happened. Brian's got mixed up in a murder.'

'Both of you sit down.' Appleby looked with considerably more interest at Mr Button than at his son. B.B. too was out of breath. But B.B. was also as pale as death. The lad—Appleby said to himself—is clean out of his comfortable academic depth. 'And might it be described'—Appleby asked aloud—'as a particularly gruesome murder?'

'Moderately,' Bobby replied judiciously. 'You see—'

'In Oxford?'

'Yes, of course. We've driven straight over. And you've damn well got to come and clear it up.'

'But, Bobby, it isn't my business to clear up homicides in Oxford: not even in the interest of B.B. Of course, I can be told about it.'

'Well, it seems to have been like this—'

'By B.B. himself, please. It will do him good. So do you go and fetch us drinks. And, Brian, go ahead.'

'Thank you, sir—thank you very much.' Mr Button clearly liked being called Brian for a change; it braced him. 'Perhaps you know the job I've been given. It's ordering and cataloguing the Cannongate Papers.'

'The Third Marquis's stuff?'

'Yes. I'm the Cannongate Lecturer.'

'You lecture on the Papers?'

'Of course not.' B.B. found this a foolish question. 'That's just what I'm called, since I've got to be called something. I get the whole bloody archive in order, and then it's to be edited and published in a grand way, and I shall be Number Two on the job. Quite a thing for me.'

'I'm delighted to hear it. Go on.'

'All Lord Cannongate's papers have been deposited with

the college by the trustees. Masses and masses of them—and some of them as confidential as hell.'

'State papers, do you mean?'

'Well yes—but that's not exactly the rub. There's a certain amount of purely personal and family stuff. It hasn't been sieved out. I have to segregate it and lock it up. It has nothing to do with what can ever be published.'

'Then the trustees ought to have done that job themselves.'

'I couldn't agree more. But they're lazy bastards, and the responsibility has come on me. It's a question of confidence. If there's a leak, what follows is a complete shambles, so far as my career's concerned.'

'I see.' Appleby looked with decent sympathy at this agitated young man. 'But I think something has been said about murder? That sounds rather a different order of thing.'

'Yes, of course.' B.B. passed a hand across his brow. 'A sense of proportion, and all that. I must try to get it right.' B.B. took a big breath. 'So just listen.'

And B.B. began to tell his story.

He worked, it seemed, in a kind of commodious dungeon beneath the college library. The cavernous chamber was impregnable; so, within it, were the numerous steel filing cabinets in which the Cannongate Papers had arrived. B.B., coming and going, had only to deal faithfully with locks and keys, and nothing could go wrong. Unfortunately it is not easy, when living in a residential university, to bear at all constantly in mind that the world is inhabited by others as well as scholars and gentlemen, ancient faithful manservants of a quasi-hereditary sort, a few pretty secretaries, and an excellent *chef*. One may differ sharply from one's colleagues over such issues as the problem of the historical Socrates; one may even be conscious that at times quite naked and shocking animosities can generate themselves out of less learned matters—as, for example, where to hang a picture or who shall look after the wine; but one doesn't—one simply doesn't—expect to have one's pocket picked or one's researches plagiarised. The concept of the felonious, in short, is one to which it is difficult to give serious thought.

These considerations—or something like them—B.B. did a little divagate to advance, as the early stages of his narrative now unfolded themselves. He had not always been too careful about those bloody keys, and he would look a pretty fool in a witness-box if this ghastly affair had the consequence of depositing him in one before a judge and jury.

Appleby's benevolent reception of the troubles of Bobby's friend didn't stand up to all this too well. He had a simple professional persuasion that keys exist to be turned in locks without fail at appropriate times, and that a young man who has gone vague on instructions he has received and accepted in such a matter ought not to be let off being told that he has been improperly negligent. On the other hand it was possible that B.B. was himself feeling very bad indeed. These were considerations that required balanced utterance.

'I hope,' Appleby said, 'that we needn't conclude your culpable carelessness over these things to have been the direct occasion of somebody's getting murdered. It sounds inherently improbable. But go on.'

'Well, sir, there's rather a difficult one there.' B.B. was recovering from the extreme disarray in which he had arrived at Dream. 'I suppose the original chunk of dirty work—a bit of thieving—couldn't have happened if I'd always been right on the ball over those rotten keys. But the murder's a different matter. That seems to have been the result of my having, as a matter of fact, a brighter moment.'

'Brian saw the significance of the electricity.' Bobby Appleby, who had returned to his father's study deftly carrying a decanter, three glasses and a plate of chocolate biscuits, offered this luminous remark. 'Absolutely top-detective stuff, if you ask me.'

'But I don't ask you. So just pour us that sherry and be quiet.' Appleby turned back to Mr Button. 'More about your brighter moment, please.'

'When I happen on any paper dealing with a certain delicate and purely family matter, I have instructions to photocopy it. There's some prospect of a law-suit, it seems, over whether a grandson of *my* Lord Cannongate was of legitimate birth or not; and a sort of dossier has to be got together for some solicitors.'

'You have to make only one copy?'

'Yes—and when I came on something relevant earlier this week I did just that. We have a machine on which we can do the job ourselves, you see, in one of the college offices. There were eight pages of the stuff, and when I'd made a copy I filed the eight sheets of it away in a special box with other photocopies of similar material. That was on Monday. Yesterday morning I had to go to that box again, and I happened to turn over those particular copies. Only, the sheets were pretty well stuck to each other still. So you see.'

'No, Brian, I *don't* see.' Appleby glanced from the Cannongate Lecturer to the creator of *The Lumber Room* (who was punishing the chocolate biscuits rather more heavily than the sherry). He might have been wondering whether England was exclusively populated by excessively clever young men. 'Why should they be stuck to each other?'

'Because of what Bobby says—the electricity.' B.B. seemed surprised that this had not been immediately apparent. 'Those photocopying machines are uncommonly lavish with it. Static electricity, I think it's called. If you stack your copies one on top of another as they come out of the contraption, they cling to one another like—'

'Like characters in a skin-flick.' Bobby had momentarily stopped munching to offer this helpful simile. 'And that's what Brian found.'

'I see.' Appleby was no longer mystified. 'The electrical phenomenon fades, and therefore the sheets manifesting it yesterday could not be those which you had filed away on Monday. Earlier yesterday, or just a little before that, somebody had extracted your copies from their box; photocopied them in turn; and then—inadvertently, perhaps—returned to the box not the older copies but the newer ones. And, but for this curious electrical or magnetic effect on the paper, and but for your being alert enough to notice it and draw the necessary inference, nobody need ever have known that there had been any monkey-business at all.'

'That's it, sir. And, if I may say so, pretty hot of you to get there in one.'

'Thank you very much,' Appleby said a shade grimly. 'It doesn't exactly tax the intellect. And just what did you do, Brian, when you made this unfortunate discovery?'

'I went straight to our Master, Robert Durham, and told him the whole thing. There was nothing else for it but to confess to the head man.'

'That was thoroughly sensible of you.' Appleby spoke as a man mollified. 'And how has the Master taken it?'

'How *did* he take it,' Bobby corrected, and reached for another biscuit.

'*What?*' Appleby looked from one to the other young man aghast. 'Brian. . .?'

'Yes, sir. You see, the Master seemed to have ideas about what had happened, although he didn't tell me what they were. It appeared to ring a bell. And that must be why they've murdered him.'

'Good God!' Appleby had a passing acquaintance with the scholar thus summarily disposed of.

'We could have better spared a better man.' Bobby offered this improving quotation with some solemnity. 'Of course, the old boy had had his life. I did feel that. He must have been sixty, if he was a day. He'd toasted his bottom before the fire of life. It sank—'

'Possibly so.' Appleby made no attempt to find this out-of-turn mortuary humour diverting, but he did perhaps judge it, from Bobby, a shade mysterious.

'Still,' Bobby went on, 'even if the Master was a clear case for euthanasia, the thing must be cleared up. *You* must come and clear it up, as I've said. The fact is, they may be getting round to imagining things.'

'Who do you mean by "they"? B.B. seems to be applying the word to a gang of assassins.'

'What *I* mean is the police.' Bobby Appleby was suddenly speaking slowly and carefully. 'They may pitch on some quite unsuitable suspect. For instance, on B.B. himself. You see, there are one or two things you haven't yet heard.'

'To my confusion, Bobby means.' Mr Button, who had cheered up while retailing his acumen over the electrified photocopies, was again sunk in gloom, and he had blurted this out after a short expressive silence. 'I think the police believe I took the Master a cock-and-bull story, just as a cover-up for something else. I think they believe the Master spotted my deception, and that I killed him because otherwise I'd have been turfed out in disgrace and it would have been the end of me.'

'That's a succinct statement, at least.' Appleby was looking at his son's friend gravely. 'Does it mean that, in addition to being careless with those keys, you had been at fault in some other way as well?'

'I'm afraid it does. You see, I'd had the idea of writing a few popular articles on the side.'

'My dear young man! You were going to publicise this intimate Cannongate family scandal you've been talking about?'

'Of course not!' B.B. had flushed darkly. 'Just some purely political things. I'd have got permission, and all that, from the trustees. But I felt I wanted to have a definite proposition to put to them. So I had a newspaper chap up from London several times, and showed him this and that. It was a bit irregular, I suppose. It could have looked bad. As a matter of fact, our senior History Tutor came on us a couple of times, and didn't seem to like it. I expect he has told the pigs.'

'As it had undoubtedly now become his duty to do.'

Appleby wasn't pleased by this manner of referring to the police. 'But this London contact of yours could at least substantiate your comparatively blameless intentions?'

'I suppose so.'

'On the other hand, if this journalist is an unscrupulous person, might he have come back into the college and done this thieving and copying himself? Had you told him about those more intimate papers? Even shown them to him?'

'Not shown them. And only mentioned them in a general way. A bit of talk over a pint. He may have gathered where they were kept.'

'Could he, as a stranger, have got swiftly at the photo-copying machine?'

'Well, yes—in theory. I took him in there and copied something trivial for him—just to show him we're quite up to date. It's all a bit unfortunate.'

'I agree. And is there anything else that's unfortunate? For example, have you done any other indiscreet talking about this scandal-department in the Cannongate Papers?'

'No, of course not. Or only to Bruno.'

'Very well, B.B. Tell me about Bruno.'

'Bruno Bone is our English Tutor, although he's pretty well just a contemporary of Bobby and me. Teaches Words-worth and Coleridge and all that sort of stuff. But, really, he wants to be a novelist. More junk yards, so to speak.' This impertinent glance at Bobby's masterpiece was accompanied by rather a joyless laugh on B.B.'s part. 'I told Bruno one evening that there was a whole novel in those damned private papers.'

'That was sheer nonsense, I suppose?'

'I'm afraid so. You know how it is, late at night and after some drinks. Talking for effect, and all that.'

'But at least your brilliant conversation apprised Mr Bone that these scandalous papers exist? Did he take any further interest in them?'

'Well, yes. Bruno came in one morning and asked to have

a dekko. He was a bit huffed when I told him it couldn't be done.'

'Just how did you tell him?'

'Oh, I slapped the relevant box and said "Not for you, my boy".'

'I see.' Appleby gazed in some fascination at this un-believably luckless youth. 'Tell me, B.B. Of course there isn't the material for a novel in your wretched dossier. But might there be material for blackmail?'

'Definitely, I'd say. It's not all exactly past history, you know. There are still people alive—'

'All right—we needn't go into details yet. But tell me this: might the Master have got to know about your chatter to Bruno Bone?'

'It's not unlikely. Bruno's an idiot. Talk about anything to anybody.'

'That's a habit I'm glad to feel you disapprove of. Do you think Bruno could have developed some morbid and irrational curiosity as a result of all this, and have actually abstracted that particular bunch of papers and made copies of them?'

'I suppose it's possible. Those literary characters are wildly neurotic.'

'And the Master might have found out—with the result that Bruno's own career would suddenly have been very much at risk?'

'Yes. The Master is—was—rather a dab at nosing things out.'

'And that brings us to the last relevant point at the moment. Just how did Dr Durham die?'

'Brains blown out.' Bobby Appleby (who had finished the last chocolate biscuit) produced this robustly. 'With some sort of revolver, it seems. Not something it's likely that Brian keeps handy, I'd have thought.'

'Nor Bruno,' B.B. said handsomely.

'Nor any stray blackmailer, either.' Appleby was frowning.

'You wouldn't know whether the police are claiming to have found the weapon?'

'Oh, yes.' Bobby nodded vigorously. 'It was just lying on the carpet in the Master's study.'

'That's where I'd expect it to be.' Appleby sounded faintly puzzled. 'You know, the great majority of men who are found with their brains blown out have effected the messy job themselves. And even in the moment of death some spasm or convulsion can result in the weapon's landing yards away. So, just for the moment, this story of yours sounds to me something of a mare's nest. Robert Durham is in some pathological state of depression and suddenly makes away with himself. And then in comes Brian's bad conscience about his handling of his archive. Bobby, wouldn't you agree? You've said something that makes me think you would agree.'

'Have I?' Bobby seemed not to make much of this. 'Durham wasn't *my* Master, you know. He got the job only when mine died a couple of years ago. But I've seen enough of him to know that he was a rum bird.'

'Secretive,' B.B. added. 'Nobody quite knew what he was up to. He was a bit remote. Brooding type. And a sick man, some said.'

'God bless my soul!' As he made use of this antique expression, Sir John Appleby got to his feet. 'Unless you're both having me up the garden path, you're describing a thoroughly persuasive candidate for suicide. Not that such don't get murdered from time to time. They may ingeniously elect liquidation in one way or another, without so much as being conscious of the fact. Which is psychologically interesting, no doubt, but murder it nevertheless remains.' Appleby paused, and looked searchingly from one young man to the other. 'Is there anything else I ought to know?'

'Not in the way of fact, I'd say.' For the moment, Bobby Appleby (so childishly addicted to chocolate biscuits) appeared to have taken charge of things. 'Of course, the people who may have extra facts are the police. And they *do* have something. I don't know what—but I know it's there. I was present when they talked to Brian early this morning. They kept mum, but I knew they had *something*.' Bobby grinned at his father. 'Family instinct, perhaps. It's why I brought Brian over to Dream. You *can* take a hand?'

'I can stroll around the college, and have a chat here and there. I'd tell the Chief Constable, and he wouldn't mind a bit—always provided I was tactful with his men on the spot. And being *that* is one of the things I keep a grip on even in senescence.' Appleby, as he momentarily adopted this humorous vein, let his glance stray out of the window. It fixed itself briefly, and then returned to the two young men. 'I'll make a call or two,' he said easily, and moved towards the door. 'Drink up the sherry meanwhile : there's about a thimbleful left for each of you.'

With this, Appleby left the room. But he was back before much in the way of telephone-calls could have been achieved.

'We were talking about the police,' he said gently. 'As a matter of fact, they're here; and—Brian—they very probably have a warrant for your arrest.'

'The personalities of the people concerned?' The Vice-Master, who was called Fordyce, looked at Appleby doubt-fully. 'That's not what the local police are asking. They want to know who had keys to what, and when who could have been where.'

'Quite right. Absolutely essential.' Appleby nodded approvingly. 'It's what gets the results—in nine cases out of ten. And, on this occasion, they appear to have got a result quite rapidly. Too rapidly, I think you'd say?'

'Of course I'd say. The notion of that young man Brian Button providing himself with a revolver and shooting the Master dead with it in his own study is simply too fantastic to stand up.'

'But just at the moment, Vice-Master, it seems to be

standing up rather well. The police have no doubt about what Dr Durham was doing when he was shot down—and it's what they've discovered that has led them to question our young man. Durham was dictating a letter on his tape-recorder for his secretary to type out later. It was to the Cannongate trustees, and said flatly that Button had been guilty of professional misconduct of so scandalous a sort that he must be dismissed at once—even although it meant that all academic employment would henceforth be closed to him.'

'It was a very strange thing for the Master to propose to write, Sir John.'

'Well, there it is. The tape isn't to be denied. The Master appears to have flicked the switch that stops the machine simply because he was interrupted while on the job. So the record remained for the police to find.'

'I understand the police case. Button has admitted going to see the Master early yesterday morning and telling him a story about rifled papers. It is now supposed that he returned again in the late afternoon, armed and resolved. The Master told him of the step he proposed to take, but without saying that he had at that moment broken off from recording his letter. So Button killed him, hoping thus to smother up the whole thing. I repeat that it is utter nonsense, completely alien to Brian Button's character, such as it is. A somewhat irresponsible young man, perhaps. But not precisely bloody, bold, and resolute.'

'It's Durham's character that interests me more. And aren't you saying that he too seems to have behaved *out* of character?'

'In a sense, that is so.' Fordyce had taken this point soberly. 'But perhaps I have to say that, although I knew Robert Durham long before he became Master, I never quite understood the man. I have sometimes thought of him as harbouring that degree of inner instability which is liable to produce what they call a personality-change. And yet that is a fantastic speculation.'

'At least a change of job, one supposes, may bring out something roughly of that sort. Was there any particular regard in which he appeared to you to be changing?'

'I can scarcely answer that without appearing very much at sea, Sir John. In one aspect Durham was a man growing detached, remote, fatigued. In another, he was becoming irascible, authoritarian, and increasingly prone to flashes of odd behaviour. He could behave like an old-fashioned headmaster with a vindictive turn of mind.'

'Dear me! That sort of thing surely doesn't cut much ice with undergraduates today?'

'Decidedly not. They can be a very great nuisance, our young men. But it is reason alone that is of any avail with them. It's something they have a little begun to get the hang of. Talk sense patiently enough and without condescension— and round they always come.' Fordyce had delivered this high doctrine with an effect of sudden intellectual conviction. 'Durham had lost grip on that.'

'How did he get along with the younger dons?'

'Ah! Not too well.'

'To the extent of anything like feud? With Button himself, for instance?'

'With Button, I'd scarcely suppose so—although the lad may have annoyed him. Nor with any of them to what you might call a point of naked animosity. Bone might be an exception.'

'Bone? A young man called Bruno Bone?'

'Yes. I'm not sure that Bone, for whatever reason, hadn't got to the point of hating Durham in his guts.' It was rather unexpectedly that the Vice-Master had produced this strong expression.

'But Bone, too, would scarcely be bloody, bold, and resolute?'

'Of course not. He—' The Vice-Master, who seemed to

have produced this reply by rote, suddenly checked himself. 'Do you know,' he said, 'that I wouldn't be quite confident of that? But then I'm coming to wonder what I shall ever be robustly confident about again. This is an undermining affair, Sir John.'

But Bone, a lanky, prematurely bald young man, was spending his Saturday afternoon banging away on his typewriter. Perhaps he was writing a lecture, or perhaps he was writing a novel. Whichever it was, he didn't seem much to care for being interrupted by the mere father of the author of *The Lumber Room*.

'Yes, of course I know they've arrested Button,' Bone said. 'So what?'

'I'd rather suppose you might be distressed or concerned. Not that they have, perhaps, quite arrested him. He's helping them with their inquiries. They have to tread carefully, you know. But it's true they hold a document from a magistrate. It's in reserve. But I'd simply like to ask, Mr Bone, what you think of the affair.'

'Absolute poppycock. Brian Button's an irresponsible idiot, and I wouldn't trust him with looking after the beer in the buttery, let alone those Cannongate Papers. But he wouldn't shoot old bloody Durham. Wouldn't have the nerve.'

'Would you?'

'If you weren't old enough to be my father, I'd tell you that was a damned impertinent question.'

'Never mind the impertinence. Would you?'

'I don't know that I know.' Bruno Bone was of a sudden entirely amenable. 'It's an interesting speculation. On the whole—I'm ashamed to say—I guess not.'

'Or would anybody else in the college?'

'Can't think of anybody.'

'Then I'm left—so far as anybody who has been put a name to goes—with a London journalist whom Button sent for and talked to a shade rashly. There are journalists, I suppose, who are fit for anything.'

'This one may have scented a hopeful whiff of blackmail, or something of that kind? And the Master may have got on to what he was up to, and had his brains blown out for his pains? I wouldn't like to have to render such a course of events plausible in a novel.'

'If you ever try, I'll hope to read your attempt at it.' Appleby gave this quite a handsome sound. 'When did you last see Dr Durham?'

'When did I last see my father?' Bruno Bone was amused. 'Quite late in the day, really. I'm not a bad suspect, come to think of it. Smart of you to be chasing me up, Sir John. Quite Bobby's father, if I may say so. Bobby's bright.'

'I never judged him exactly dim—but the point's not of the first relevance. Be more precise, please.'

'Very well. I went to see the old brute about an hour before he was indubitably dead. Probably the last man in, so to speak. A breathless hush in the close, and all that. I wanted to sound him out about the prospects of my touching the college for a travel grant. California. Awful universities, but a marvellous climate. Durham treated me as if I was a ghost. Bizarre, wouldn't you say? Considering he was so well on the way to becoming one himself.'

'No doubt. What was the Master doing?'

'Concocting a letter.'

'On some sort of dictaphone?'

'Nothing of the sort. Laborious pen and ink. And putting a lot of concentration into it, I'd say. He made a civil pretence of listening to me for about thirty seconds, and then turfed me out. He was back on his job before I'd reached the door.'

'And that was the last you saw of him?'

'No, it wasn't.' Bruno Bone was sardonically triumphant. 'And here's where I get off the hook. I saw him ten minutes later—and so must plenty of other people—crossing the great quadrangle, with his letter in his hand. He went out through the main gate, crossed the road to the post office, shoved his letter into the box, and came back.'

'There would be nothing particularly out of the way, would there, about all that?'

'Of course there would. He had only to leave the thing on a table in his hall, and it would have been collected and dealt with by a college messenger.'

'Thank you very much, Mr Bone. And I apologise for disturbing you.'

Appleby's final call was on the senior History Tutor, an elderly man called Farnaby. Farnaby, he supposed, was in some vague and informal fashion Brian Button's boss.

'One of Button's indiscretions,' Appleby said, 'appears to have been dreaming up some popular articles based on the documents in his charge, and calling in a man from some paper or other with whom to discuss the matter. Would you term his doing that a grave breach of confidence?'

'Certainly not. Button ought, no doubt, to have mentioned the proposal to the Master or to myself in the first instance. It might even be said that there was a slight element of discourtesy in his conduct of the matter; and anything of the kind is, of course, greatly to be deprecated in a society like ours.'

'Of course.'

'But let us simply call it an error of judgement. Button has the makings of a competent scholar; but of what may be called *practical* judgement he has very little sense.'

'I see. Would you say, Dr Farnaby, that the young man's lack of practical judgement might extend to his supposing it judicious to murder Dr Durham?'

'Of course not. I am almost inclined, Sir John, to say that the question could be asked only in a frivolous spirit. It is utter nonsense.'

'So everybody except the police appears to feel. Might Button be described as a protégé of yours?'

'I don't think we go in for protégés.' Farnaby had frowned. 'But I certainly feel in some degree responsible for him. He was my pupil, and it was I who recommended him for his present employment.'

'Thank you. Now, it appears to me, Dr Farnaby, that we have at present just one hard fact in this affair. The day before yesterday, or thereabout, some person unknown abstracted eight sheets from a file of photocopies, photocopied those photocopies anew, and then returned the newer and not the older photocopies to the file. The switch was almost certainly fortuitous rather than intentional. It could not have been designed to attract Button's attention, since there was no particular likelihood of his turning over those particular papers again before the static electricity had faded from them. At this specific point, then, we have no reason to suspect any sort of plot against the young man.'

'Clearly not.'

'Button went to the Master and told his story. The Master —if Button is to be believed, and if he didn't form a false impression—the Master responded to the story as if he had some inkling of what lay behind it. It rang a bell. That is Button's phrase for it. Does that suggest anything to you?'

'Nothing whatever, I fear.'

'I suppose everybody would have learnt almost at once about Button's cleverness in tumbling to the implications of that small electrical phenomenon?'

'Almost certainly. He's a young man who can't help chattering.'

'Do you think that his chatterbox quality, and perhaps other forms of tiresomeness, may have been irritating the Master in a manner, or to a degree, Button himself wasn't aware of?'

'I'm afraid it is only too probable. Poor Durham was becoming rather intolerant of folly.'

'That seems to be a view generally held—and it brings me to my last point. The Vice-Master has given me some impression of Durham as a man. And he judges it rather odd, for one thing, that Durham should have thought to dictate a letter to the Cannongate trustees that could only have resulted in Button's being sacked. But again—and rather contradictorily—he represents Durham as increasingly irascible, indeed vindictive. How would you yourself describe the man?'

'He owned a certain complexity of character, I suppose. Sit beside him at dinner, and you might judge him rather a dull—even a morose man, particularly during his recent ill-health. But in solitude and at his desk he must have become something quite different, since his writing was often brilliantly witty. And maliciously witty, it may be added; whereas in all his college relations his sense of the academic proprieties extended almost to the rectitudinous.' Farnaby paused, and seemed to become aware of this speech as a shade on the heavy side. 'In fact,' he added, 'poor Robert Durham, barring occasional acts of almost alarming eccentricity, was a bit of a bore. But it would have been a safe bet that the memoirs he was working on would have been highly entertaining. You will recall that he was in political life as a younger man, and knew everybody there was to know. It was probably because he found Oxford a bit of a bore that *we* found *him* one. But I must not speak uncharitably. A horrifying mystery like this is a chastening thing.'

'It is, no doubt, horrifying.' Appleby stood up. 'Or, if not horrifying, at least distressing. Whether it is a mystery is another matter. We can only wait and see.'

'Wait and see, Sir John! I very much hope that the most active steps are being taken to clear the matter up.'

'In a sense, perhaps they are. A little patience is what is required, all the same.'

'And my unfortunate young colleague has to set us an

example in the matter?' Farnaby spoke with asperity. 'Button has to rest content in his cell?'

'I think not. It is improbable that any very definitive step has been taken in regard to him. Perhaps I can make myself useful—in this way if in no other, my dear sir—by persuading my former colleagues to part with him. In fact, I'll take him back to Dream with me. He and Bobby can play tennis.'

'And for how long will they have to do *that*?' Although he uttered this question challengingly, Farnaby was clearly much relieved.

'Oh, until Monday morning. It's my guess that between breakfast and lunch on that day Dr Durham's demise will effectively clear itself up.'

And it was at ten o'clock on Monday that Appleby strolled out to the tennis court. A police car had arrived at Dream and departed again, and Appleby now had some papers in his hand.

'Relax,' he said to the two young men. 'Your late Master wilfully sought his own salvation. Or that's how the First Grave Digger would put it. *Felo de se*. The letter has arrived, and all is clear.'

'The letter?' Brian Button repeated. 'The one he was dictating—'

'No, no, B.B. Have some sense, my dear boy. The one your friend Bruno came on him writing, and that he took over to the post office himself. Stamped, of course, as second-class mail.'

'I don't understand you, sir.' B.B. had sat down on a garden seat; he was almost as pale as when he had arrived at Dream in the first instance.

'And I'm blessed if I do either.' Bobby Appleby chucked his tennis racket on the grass at his feet. 'Explain—for goodness sake.'

'Come, come—where's all that absolutely top-detective stuff?' Appleby was in irritatingly good humour. 'And,

Bobby, you had an instinct it was all a matter of Durham's calling it a day: don't you remember your prattle about the fire of life, and euthanasia, and whatever? As for the letter, it stared us in the face. The Master didn't want it to go out of his lodging through the college messenger service, so he took it to the post himself.'

'He was anxious,' B.B. demanded, 'to conceal whom he was writing to?'

'Not exactly that. *The letter was to somebody in college.* And he didn't want to risk its being delivered, after his death, more or less straight away by hand. Despatched by second-class mail, it would be delivered this morning. And it was. To the Vice-Master.'

'And just what was this in aid of?' It was clear from his tone that Brian Button already dimly knew.

'It was in aid, my dear lad, of what his seemingly interrupted communication to the Cannongate trustees on that tape-recorder was also in aid of. Something quite extravagantly malevolent. For let's face it, B.B. You'd annoyed him. You'd annoyed him quite a lot. And he was maliciously resolved to make his departure from this life the occasion of your experiencing *un mauvais quart d'heure.* Or rather more.'

'He thought it was really me who had done that monkeying with the photocopies?'

'No B.B. He couldn't have thought that. For the Master had done that copying turn himself. Incidentally, the photocopying machine has been in use this morning. By the police. And they've sent me out this.' Appleby handed a paper to B.B. 'From the Master to the Vice-Master. Robert Durham's testament, poor chap.'

My dear Adrian,

First, let me say how much I hope that the Fellows will elect you into the Mastership. If it should come about that I am permitted to look down upon the college from on high, or obliged to peer up at it from below, this will be the spectacle I shall most wish to view. Bless you, my dear man.

Secondly, pray have the police release that wretched Button. (Is not this appropriately reminiscent of some of the last words of Shakespeare's Lear?) If he be not in custody as you read this, it is because they have been so stupid and negligent as to neglect the tape-recorder on my desk. But surely not even Dogberry and Verges could be so dull.

Button needs a lesson in (as we used to say) pulling his socks up. He is also (what, most illogically, I cannot quite forgive him) the immediate occasion of the step I am about to take. The Cannongate Papers contain some fascinating things, and the censurable carelessness of this young man prompted me to help myself in a clandestine fashion to certain material useful to—shall I say—a historian of the intimate *mores* of the more elevated classes of society at least not very long ago. Unfortunately the beastly Button is very acute; he detected the theft, and came to tell me about it with a mingling of trepidation, uneasiness, complacency and self-congratulation which has extremely offended me.

I need not speak of my present state of health. What has told me that the time has come is really, and precisely, this Button business. *He* hasn't found me out but *I* have found *myself* out. And in an action of the weirdest eccentricity! As that equally tiresome Bruno Bone would tell you, the poet Pope speaks of Heads of Houses who beastly Skelton quote. But who ever heard of a Head of a House given to petty nocturnal pilferings?

Ave, Hadriane, moriturus te salutat.

ROBERT DURHAM
Master

THE MEMORIAL SERVICE

I N   T H E   F A S H I O N A B L E   church of St Boniface in the
Fields (mysteriously so named, since it was in the heart of
London) a large and distinguished congregation was
assembled to give thanks for the life of the late Christopher
Brockbank Q.C. The two newspaper reporters at the door,
discreetly clad in unjournalistic black, had been busy receiving and recording all sorts of weighty names. It was the sort
of occasion upon which sundry persons explain themselves as
'representing' sundry other persons even more august than
themselves; or sundry institutions, corporations, charities and
learned bodies with which the deceased important individual
has been associated.

Legal luminaries predominated. An acute observer (and
there was at least one such present) might have remarked that
a number of these did not settle in their pews, kneel, and
bury their noses devoutly in their cupped hands without an
exchange of glances in which a hint of whimsical humour
fleetingly flickered. *All this for Chris Brockbank!* they appeared to be telling each other. *Just what would he have
made of it?*

Sir John Appleby (our acute observer) was representing
his successor as Commissioner of Metropolitan Police. For
Brockbank long ago, and before he had transformed himself
from a leading silk into a vigorous and somewhat eccentric
legal reformer, had owned his connections with Scotland
Yard, and this fact had to be duly acknowledged today.
Appleby possessed only a vague memory of the man, so that
a certain artificiality perhaps attended his presence at the
service. It hadn't seemed decent, however, to decline a

135

request which was unlikely to occupy him for much more than twenty minutes—or thirty-five if one counted the time spent in scrambling into uniform and out again.

It would have been hard to tell that it wasn't something quite different—even a wedding—that was about to transact itself. Gravity now and then there had to be, but on the whole a cheerful demeanour is held not improper on such occasions. The good fight has been fought, and nothing is here for tears, nothing to wail or knock the breast. Six weeks had passed, moreover, since Christopher Brockbank's death, and anybody much stunned by grief had thus had a substantial period in which to recover. Whether there had been many such appeared doubtful. Brockbank had been unmarried, and now the front pew reserved for relations was occupied only by two elderly women, habited in old-fashioned and no doubt frequently exhibited mourning, whom some-body had identified for Appleby in a whisper as cousins of the dead man. If anything, they appeared rather to be enjoy-ing their role. It was to be conjectured that they owned some quite obscure, although genteel, situation in society. Nobody had ever heard of any Brockbanks until Christopher Q.C. had come along. In some corner of the globe, Appleby vaguely understood, there was a brother, Adrian Brockbank, who had also distinguished himself—it seemed as a lone yachtsman. But the wandering Adrian had not, it seemed, hoisted himself into a jet for the occasion.

The congregation had got to its feet, and was listening to the singing of a psalm. It was well worth listening to, since the words were striking in themselves and the choir of St Boniface's is justly celebrated. The congregation was, of course, in the expectation of playing a somewhat passive part. At such services it is understood that there is to be compara-tively little scope for what, in another context, would be called audience participation.

Appleby looked about him. It was impressive that the Lord Chief Justice had turned up, and that he was flanked by two Ministers of the Crown. There were also two or three socially prominent dowagers, who were perhaps recalling passages with Christopher when he had been young as well as gay : these glanced from time to time in benevolent amusement at the two old creatures in the front pew. Among the clergy, and wearing a very plain but very golden pectoral cross, was a bishop who would presently ascend the pulpit and deliver a brief address. In the nave two elderly clubmen (as they ought probably to be called) of subdued raffish appearance were putting their heads together in muttered colloquy. These must liaise with yet another aspect of the dead man's dead life. They were presumably laying a wager with one another on just how many minutes the address would occupy.

The service proceeded with unflawed decorum. An anthem was sung. The bishop, ceremoniously conducted to his elevated perch, began his address. He lost no time in launching upon a character-analysis of the late Queen's Counsel; it would have been possible to imagine an hour-glass of the diminutive sort used for nicely timing the boiling of eggs as being perched on the pulpit's edge beside him. The analysis, although touching lightly once or twice upon endearing foible, was highly favourable in the main. The dead man, disposed in his private life to charity, humility, gentleness, and the study of English madrigals, had in his professional character been dedicated, stern, courageous, and passionately devoted to upholding, clarifying, reforming his country's laws.

It was now that something slightly untoward occurred. A late arrival entered the church. An elderly man with a finely trimmed grey moustache, he was dressed with the exactest propriety for the occasion; that he was accustomed to such appearances was evident in the mere manner in which he contrived to carry a black silk hat, an umbrella, and a pair of grey kid gloves dexterously in his left hand while receiving from the hovering verger the printed service-sheet. Not many of those present thought it becoming to turn their heads to see what was happening. But nobody, in fact, was cheated of a sight of the newcomer for long. He might have been expected (however accustomed to some position of prominence) to slip modestly into a pew near the west door. But this he did not do. He walked with quiet deliberation up the central aisle—very much (Appleby thought) as if he were an integral and expected part of the ritual which he was in fact indecorously troubling. He walked right up to the front pew, and sat down beside Christopher Brockbank's female relatives.

There could be only one explanation. Here was the missing Adrian, brother of the dead man—to whom, indeed, Appleby's recollection sufficed to recognise that he bore a strong family likeness. Perhaps the plane from Singapore or the Bahamas or wherever had been delayed; perhaps fog had caused it to be diverted from Heathrow to a more distant airport; thus rendered unavoidably tardy in his appearance, this much-travelled Brockbank had decided that he must afford a general indication of his presence, and move to the support of the ladies of the family, even at the cost of rendering an effect of considerable disturbance. It must have been—Appleby thought sympathetically—a difficult decision to make.

The address went on. The new arrival listened with close attention to what must now be the tail-end of it. And everybody else ought to have been doing the same thing.

But this was not so. The Lord Chief Justice had hastily removed one pair of spectacles, donned another, and directed upon the fraternal appearance in the front pew the kind of gaze which for many years he had been accustomed to bring to bear upon occupants of the dock at the Central Criminal Court. One of the Cabinet Ministers was looking frightened —which is something no Cabinet Minister should ever do. Two of the dowagers were talking to one another in agitated and semi-audible whispers. A third appeared to be on the verge of hysterics. As for the bishop, he was so upset that he let the typescript of his carefully prepared allocution flutter to the floor below, with the result that he was promptly reduced to a preoration in terms of embarrassed improvisation.

But before even this was concluded, the brother—whether veritable or supposititious—of the late Christopher Brockbank behaved very strangely. He stood up, moved into the aisle, and bowed. He bowed, not towards the altar (which would have been very proper in itself), but at the bishop in his pulpit (and this wasn't proper at all). He then turned, and retreated as he had come. Only, whereas on arriving he had kept his eyes decently directed upon the floor, on departing he bowed to right and left as he walked—much like a monarch withdrawing from an audience-chamber through a double file of respectful courtiers. He paused only once, and that was beside the uniformed Appleby, upon whom he directed a keen but momentary glance, before politely handing him his service-sheet. Then he resumed his stately progress down the aisle until he reached the church-door and vanished.

Somebody would possibly have followed a man so patently deranged, and therefore conceivably a danger to himself or others, had not the Rector of St Boniface's thought it expedient to come to the rescue of the flustered bishop by promptly embarking upon the prayers which, together with a hymn, were to conclude the service. These prayers (which are full of tremendous things) it would have been indecent to disturb. But a hymn is only a hymn, and it was quite plain that numerous members of the congregation were giving utterance not to the somewhat jejune sentiments this one proposed to them, but to various expressions, delivered more or less *sotto voce*, of indignation and stupefaction. The Lord Chief Justice, moreover, was gesturing. He was gesturing at Appleby in a positively threatening way which Appleby perfectly understood. If Appleby bolted from this untoward and unseemly incident instead of reacting to it in some policemanlike fashion he would pretty well be treated as in contempt of court. This was why he found himself standing on the pavement outside St Boniface's a couple of minutes later.

'Get into this thing,' the Lord Chief Justice said imperiously, and pointed at his Rolls Royce. 'You, too,' he said to the Home Secretary (who was one of the two Ministers who had been giving thanks for the life of the deceased Brockbank). 'We can't let such an outrage pass.'

'An outrage?' Appleby queried, as he resignedly sat down in the car. 'Wasn't it merely that Christopher Brockbank's brother is mildly dotty—nothing more?'

'Adrian merely dotty! Damn it, Appleby, didn't you realise what he was doing? He was *impersonating* Christopher—nothing less. That moustache, those clothes, his entire bearing: they weren't remotely Adrian. They were Christopher *tout court*. Didn't you remark the reaction of those who knew Christopher well? Both those Brockbank brothers were given to brutal and tasteless practical jokes, but this has been the most brutal and tasteless of the lot.'

'They may well have been. In fact, I seem to remember hearing something of the sort about them. But if Adrian has judged it funny to get himself up like Christopher in order to attend Christopher's memorial service that seems to me entirely his own affair. I shall be surprised, Pomfret, if you can tell me he has broken the law.' Appleby smiled at the eminent judge. 'Although, of course, it wouldn't at all do for me not to believe what you say.'

'I don't believe it was Adrian at all. It was Christopher's ghost.' The Home Secretary endeavoured to offer this in a whimsical manner. It was he who had been looking patently frightened ten minutes before, and he was endeavouring to carry this off lightly now. 'Turn up as a ghost for something like one's own funeral is a joke good enough to gratify any purgatorial spirit, I'd suppose. What we've witnessed is the kind of thing those psychic chaps call a veridical phantasm of the dead.'

'I haven't set eyes on Christopher Brockbank for thirty years,' Appleby said, 'and his wandering brother Adrian I've never seen at all. This well-groomed person bowing himself down the aisle in that crazy fashion was *very* like Christopher?'

'Very.'

'Thoroughly scandalous,' Lord Pomfret said. 'Not to be tolerated. Appleby, you must look into it.'

'My dear Chief Justice, I have no standing in such matters. This uniform is merely ornamental. I'm a retired man, as you know.'

'Come, come.' The Home Secretary laid a hand on Appleby's arm in a manner designed as wholly humorous. 'Do as you're told, my boy.'

'Do you know—perhaps I will? The ghost, or whatever, did a little distinguish me, after all. He stopped and handed me this.' Appleby was still holding a superfluous service-sheet. 'It was almost as if he was passing me the ball.'

Much in the way of hard fact about Christopher Brockbank turned out not easy to come by. He proved to have been surprisingly wealthy. As the elder of the two brothers he had inherited a substantial fortune, and to this he had added a second fortune earned at the Bar. Uninterested in becoming a judge, he had retired comparatively early, and for the greater part of the year lived in something like seclusion in the south of France. It was understood by his acquaintance that this was in the interest of uninterrupted labour on a work of jurisprudence directed to some system of legal reform. The accident in which he had lost his life had been a large-scale air disaster in the Alpes-Maritimes. He had died intestate, and his affairs were going to take a good deal of clearing up.

It was on the strength of no more than this amount of common knowledge, together with only a modicum of private inquiry, that Appleby eventually called upon a bank manager in the City.

'I understand from an official source,' he began blandly, 'that the late Mr Brockbank kept his private account in this country at your branch.'

'That is certainly true.' The bank manager nodded amiably. He had very clear views, Appleby conjectured, on what information was confidential and what was not. 'He used to spare a few minutes to chat with me upon the occasion of his quite infrequent visits. A delightful man.'

'No doubt. It has occurred to me that, in addition to keeping both a current and a deposit account with you, he may have been in the habit of lodging documents and so forth for safe keeping.'

'Ah.'

'I know that you maintain some sort of strong-room for such purposes, and suppose that your customers can hire strong-boxes of one convenient size or another?'

'Yes, indeed, Sir John. Should you yourself ever have occasion—'

'Thank you. Brockbank did this?'

'Sir John, may I say that, when inquiries of this sort are judged expedient for one reason or another, a request—and it can scarcely be more than a request—is commonly preferred by one of the Law Officers of the Crown?' The manager paused, and found that this produced no more than a composed nod. 'But no doubt there is little point in being sticky in the matter. Let me consult my appropriate file.' He unlocked a drawer, and rummaged. 'Yes,' he said. 'It would appear that Brockbank had such a box.'

'His executors haven't yet got round to inquiring about it?'

'Seemingly not.'

'I'd like you to open it and let me examine the contents.'

'My dear Sir John!' The manager was genuinely scandalised. 'You can scarcely believe—'

'But only in the most superficial way. I have an officer waiting in your outer office who would simply turn over these documents unopened, and apply a very simple test to the envelopes or whatever the outer coverings may prove to be. He will not take, and I shall not take, the slightest interest in what is said.'

For a moment the manager's hand hovered over his telephone. An appeal to higher authority—perhaps to the awful authority of the General Manager himself—was plainly in his mind. Then he took a deep breath.

'Very well,' he said. 'I suppose an adequate discretion will be observed?'

'Oh, most decidedly,' Appleby said.

'So that, for a start, is *that*,' Appleby murmured to the Lord Chief Justice an hour later.

'But surely, my dear Appleby, he would scarcely recognize you at a glance? The years have been passing over us, after all.'

'That is all too true. But the point isn't material. There I was, dressed up for that formal occasion in the uniform of a high-ranking officer of the Metropolitan Police. He felt he could trust me to tumble to the thing.'

'And you are quite sure? *Absolutely* sure? The fingerprints on that service-sheet were identical—'

'Beyond a shadow of doubt. Christopher Brockbank always deposited or withdrew documents from that strong-box in the presence of an official of the bank who was in a position to identify him beyond question. The man who attended Christopher Brockbank's memorial service was Christopher Brockbank himself.'

'And he wanted the fact to be known?'

'He wanted the fact to be known.'

'It makes no sense.'

'What it makes is very good *nonsense*. And there is one kind of nonsense that Brockbank is on record as having a fondness for : the kind of nonsense one calls a practical joke. And I expect he had money on it.'

'Money !' Lord Pomfret was outraged.

'Say a wager with one of his own kidney.'

'We have been most notoriously abused.' Something formidable had come into Pomfret's voice. One could almost imagine that high above his head in the chill London air the scales were trembling in the hand of the blindfolded figure of Justice which crowns the Central Criminal Court.

'I wouldn't deny it for a moment. But I come back to a point I've more or less made before. You can't send a man down, Chief Justice, for attending his own memorial service. It just isn't a crime.'

'But there must be something very like a crime in the hinterland of this impertinent buffoonery.' Lord Pomfret had flushed darkly. 'Steps have been taken to certify as dead a man who isn't dead at all.'

'In a foreign country, and in the context of some hideous and, no doubt, vastly confused air crash. Possibly without any actual knowledge of the thing on Brockbank's own part. Possibly as a consequence of innocent error—error on top of which he has merely piled an audacious joke. And a singularly tasteless joke, perhaps. But not one with gaol at the end of it.'

'We can get him. We can get him for *something*.'

'I don't know what to make of that from a legal point of view.' The retired Commissioner of Police made no bones about glancing at the Lord Chief Justice of England in frank amusement. 'And there will be a good deal of laughter in court, wouldn't you say ?'

'You're damn well right.' Not altogether unexpectedly, Lord Pomfret was suddenly laughing himself. 'But what the devil is he going to do now ? Just how is he proposing to come alive again ?'

'With great respect, m'lud, I suggest your lordship is in some confusion.' Appleby, watching his august interlocutor dive for a whisky decanter and a syphon, was laughing too. 'Christopher Brockbank *is* alive. He's in a position, so to speak, in which no further action is necessary.'

'Nor from us either? We leave him to it?'

'Just that I wouldn't say.' Appleby was grave again. 'I confess to being a little uneasy still about the whole affair.'

'The deuce you do!' Now on his feet, the Lord Chief Justice held the decanter poised in air. 'So what? Say when.'

'Only a finger,' Appleby said. 'And I'll continue to look into the thing.'

'With discretion, my dear fellow.' Pomfret was suddenly almost like the bank manager.

'Oh, most decidedly,' Appleby said.

Retired Police Commissioners don't go fossicking in France, and through the courtesy of his successor Appleby received reports in due season. Hard upon the air crash, it transpired, an elderly and distressed English gentleman had appeared upon the scene of the disaster in a chauffeur-driven car. Presenting himself to the *chef de gendarmerie* who was in control of the rescue operations, he had explained that he was Adrian Brockbank, and that he had motored straight from Nice upon hearing of the accident, since he had only too much reason to suppose that his elder brother, Mr Christopher Brockbank Q.C., had been on board the ill-fated plane. Could he be given any information about this, either way? It was explained to Mr Adrian Brockbank that much confusion inevitably prevailed; that, as often happened on such sad occasions, there was no certainty that an entirely reliable list of passengers' names existed; and that certain necessarily painful and distressing attempts at identification were even then going on. Would Mr Adrian Brockbank care . . . ?

The inquirer steeled himself, and cared. Eventually he

had been almost irrationally reluctant to admit the sad truth. A ring on the charred finger of one of the grim exhibits he had, indeed, formally to depose as being his brother's ring. But it seemed so tiny a piece of evidence! Might there not be more? A relevant article of baggage, perhaps, that had in part escaped the heat of the conflagration?

Not—it was explained to Mr Adrian Brockbank—at the moment. But something of the kind might yet turn up. As so often, debris was probably scattered over a very wide area. There was to be a systematic search at first light. With this information, Mr Adrian Brockbank and his chauffeur had departed to a near-by hotel for the night. And in the morning the sombre expectation had been fulfilled. Christopher Brockbank's briefcase had been discovered, along with other detritus, in a field nearly a quarter of a mile away; and it contained a number of recent personal papers and his passport. Whereupon Adrian, formally identifying himself through the production of his own passport and the testimony of his chauffeur, satisfied the requirements of French law by making a deposition before a magistrate. After that again, he made decent arrangements for the disposal of anything that could be called his brother's remains. And then he departed as he had come.

Such had been the highly unsatisfactory death of Christopher Brockbank.

All this, Appleby told himself, didn't remain exactly obscure once you took a straight look at it. Just as it wasn't Adrian who had turned up at the memorial service, so it hadn't been Adrian who had turned up at the grisly aftermath of that aerial holocaust. It had been Christopher on both occasions—and it was impossible to say that throughout the whole affair there had been any positive role played by Adrian at all. This was bizarre—but there was something that was mildly alarming as well. Christopher had *waited*. Equipped with a passport in the name of his brother, equipped no doubt with a duplicate passport in his own name, equipped with the briefcase which he would eventually toss into an appropriate field—equipped with all this, Christopher had waited for a sufficiently substantial disaster within, say, a couple of hours' hard motoring-distance of his French residence. He had certainly had to wait for months—and more probably for years. A thoroughly macabre pertinacity had marked the attaining of his practical joke.

And hadn't the joker overreached himself? Could any place in society remain for a man who, with merely frivolous intent, had deliberately identified an unknown dead body as his own? It seemed not surprising that Christopher hadn't been heard of again since he had walked down that aisle, graciously bowing to a bewildered congregation. Perhaps he had very justifiably lost his nerve.

But, even if Adrian didn't come into the story at all, where *was* Adrian? He was almost certainly Christopher's heir, and yet even Christopher's English solicitors appeared to know nothing about him. Perhaps they were just being more successfully cagey than that bank manager. Certainly they had, for the moment, nothing to say—except that Mr Adrian Brockbank spent most of his time sailing the seven seas.

Appleby was coming to feel, not very rationally, that time was important. He had told Lord Pomfret that he was un-easy—which had been injudicious, since he couldn't quite have explained why. Pomfret, however, had refrained from catechising him. And now he had the same feeling still. No Brockbank had died. But two Brockbanks might be described as lying low. There was about this the effect of an ominous lull.

And then Christopher Brockbank turned up.

He turned up on Appleby's urban doorstep and was shown

in—looking precisely the man who had put on the turn in
St Boniface's.

'My dear Appleby,' he said, 'I have ventured to call for
the purpose of offering you an apology.' Brockbank's address
was easy and familiar; he might have been talking to a man
he ran into every second week in one club or another.

'I don't need an apology. But I could do with an
explanation.'

'Ah, that—yes, indeed. But the apology must come first.
For dragging you into the little joke. It started up in my
mind like a creation, you know, just as I was walking out
of that church. There on the service-sheet were my fingerprints, and there were you, who if handed the thing could
be trusted to do as I have no doubt you have done. A
sublimely simple way of vindicating myself as still in the
land of the living.'

'I am delighted you are with us still.' Appleby said this
on a note of distinguishable irony. 'And I accept your
apology at once. And now, may the explanation of the little
joke follow?'

'The explanation is that it has been designed as rather
more than a little joke. My idea has been, in fact, to make a
real impact upon the complacency of some who are satisfied
with the absurd inadequacy of many of our laws. That old
fool Pomfret, for example. I have for long been a legal
reformer, after all.'

'I see.' Appleby really did see. 'This exploit has been
in the interest of high-lighting the fact, or contention, that
the law is hazardously lax in point of verifying adequately
the identity of deceased persons—that sort of thing?'

'Precisely that sort of thing. I shall have established—
strikingly because by means of an ingenious prank—that in
France and England alike—'

'Quite so, Mr Brockbank. We need not linger on the
worth of your intentions. But surely you have reflected of
late on the extent to which you are likely to be in trouble,

under French legal jurisdiction, if not under English? The deception you carried out upon the occasion of that disaster—'

'My dear Appleby, what can you be thinking of? That was my brother Adrian, was it not? This all begins from his proposing to bring off a better joke against *me* than I ever brought off against *him*. It is on the record, I suppose, that we have both rather gone in for that sort of thing. He was going to confront me with the pleasant position of being legally dead. Well, I capped his joke by, you may say, concurring. I attended—I hope in a suitably devout manner— my own memorial service. So the laugh is going to be on him.'

'Mr Brockbank, I have seldom come across so impudent an imposture!' Appleby suddenly found himself as outraged as the Lord Chief Justice had been. 'Whether your brother has, or has not, been remotely involved in this freakish and indecent affair I do not know. But I *do* know that, six weeks ago in France, you presented yourself as that brother upon an occasion at which such clowning would have been wholly inconceivable'—Appleby paused, and then took a calculated plunge—'to anybody bearing the character of a gentleman.'

'I withdraw my apology.' Christopher Brockbank had gone extremely pale. 'As for what you allege: prove it. Or get somebody with a legitimate concern in my affairs to prove it. *You* have none.'

'Then I scarcely see why you should be calling on me— except to discover how far I have penetrated to the truth of this nonsense. I am prepared to believe that you had some ghost of serious intention in the way of exposing the weakness of certain legal processes. I accept that notions of what is permissibly funny may differ as between one generation, or one coterie, and another. But your present pack of lies about the conduct of your own brother—lies which I must now suppose you to be intending to make public—is a little too steep for me. Just what are you going to say to your brother when you meet?'

'I don't quite know.' Christopher Brockbank had decided to digest the strong words which had been offered to him. 'But I must certainly decide, since I am on the point of running down to see him now.'

'I beg your pardon?' Appleby stared incredulously at his visitor.

'I said I'm off to see Adrian. I must persuade him I'm not as dead as he has tried to represent me. In a way, he doesn't know that he has not, so to speak, liquidated me quite successfully. Here is more than six weeks gone by since his little turn over my supposed body, and I haven't—so far as he knows—given a chirp. That must be puzzling him, wouldn't you say?'

'Possibly so. Do I understand that your only public appearance has been at that deplorably mistaken memorial service?'

'Yes, it has. You may simply take it that it has amused me to lie low.'

'You appear to me to be in love with your own mortality. Now more than ever seems it rich to die : that sort of thing. What if there's a general feeling, Mr Brockbank, that your decease was a welcome event? You might have quite a task in persuading a malicious world that you *are* alive; that you are *you*, in fact, and not some species of Tichborne Claimant.'

'Ah, that's where those fingerprints come in. It's hardly a piece of evidence a conscientious policeman could suppress, eh?'

'No, it is not.' Appleby was becoming impatient of this senseless conversation. 'If your brother Adrian really played that trick at the scene of the disaster—which I do not believe for a moment—he will be gratified to learn that you have taken the consequences of his joke so seriously as pretty well to register your continued existence with the police.'

'But I shan't tell him what I did with that service-sheet.' Christopher Brockbank gave a cunning chuckle. 'Not till I'm sure he hasn't got some further joke up his sleeve.' He got to his feet. 'And now I must be off to my brotherly occasion.'

'Far be it from me to detain you. But may I ask, Mr Brockbank, where your brother is to be found?'

'Ah, that will doubtless be becoming public property quite soon. Adrian is a minor celebrity in his way. But, just at the moment, I think I'll keep him to myself.'

The prediction proved accurate. The very next morning's papers carried the news that Adrian Brockbank's yacht had been sighted at anchor off Budleigh Salterton in Devon. It seemed probable that he had arrived unobtrusively in home waters several days earlier.

Appleby endeavoured to absorb this as information of only moderate interest. Christopher Brockbank had had his joke, and it had involved a breach of the law in France if not in England. He had now gone off to join his nautical brother Adrian, and crow over the manner in which he had taken Adrian's identity upon himself at the inception of the imposture in the Alpes-Maritimes. Something like that must really be what was in Christopher's mind. And it was all very far from being Appleby's business; he ought to be indifferent as to whether those two professional jokers (as they appeared to have been) decided to laugh over the thing together or to quarrel about it. Let them fight it out.

But this line of thought didn't work. Several times in the course of the morning there came back into Appleby's head one particular statement which Christopher had made. It was a statement which just *might* be fraught with a consequence not pretty to think of. At noon Appleby got out his car and drove west.

Budleigh Salterton proved not to run to a harbour. A few unimpressive craft were drawn up on a pebbly beach; far away on the horizon tankers and freighters ploughed up and down the English Channel; the sea was otherwise empty except for a single yacht riding at anchor rather far out. Binoculars didn't help to make anything of this. Where one might have been expected to read the vessel's name a tarpaulin or small sail had been spread as if to dry. Appleby appealed to a bystander.

'Do you happen to know,' he asked, 'whose yacht that is?'

'I haven't any idea.' The man addressed, although he appeared to be a resident of the place, was plainly without nautical interests. 'It has been here for some days—except that it went out at dusk yesterday evening, and I happened to see it return at dawn this morning. But I did hear somebody say there was a rumour that the fellow was one of those lone yachtsman types.'

'Do you know where I can hire a rowing-boat?'

'Just down by that groyne, I believe.'

'Thank you very much.'

'May I come on board?' Appleby called out. Adrian Brockbank was very like his brother—even down to the neat grey moustache.

'Not if you're another of those infernal journalists.'

'I'm not. I'm an infernal policeman. A retired one.'

'You can come up, if you like.' And Adrian tossed down a small accommodation ladder. He had appeared only momentarily startled.

'Thank you.' Appleby climbed, and settled himself without ceremony on the gunwale. 'Have you had any other visitors just lately, Mr Brockbank?'

'I see you know my name. Only a journalist, as I say. That was yesterday evening. But I persuaded him to clear out again.'

'What about your brother?'

'I beg your pardon?' Adrian stared.

'Your brother Christopher.'

'Good God, Mr—'

'Appleby. Sir John Appleby. Yes?'

'My brother Christopher was killed six weeks ago in an air-crash. Your question is either ignorant or outrageous.'

'That remains to be proved, sir. And I gather you have been on some extended cruise or other. Just how did you hear this sad news?'

'*Hear* it? Heaven and earth, man! It was actually I who identified Christopher's body. I'd sailed into Nice, and tried to contact him by telephone. They said he was believed to have joined a plane for Paris, and gave some particulars. Then suddenly there was the news of this—'

'So you identified the body, made certain decent arrangements about it, and then went to sea again. Is that right?'

'It is right. But I'm damned if I know what entitles you—'

'And then, only a few days ago, there was your brother's memorial service at St Boniface's in London. Do you say that you attended it?'

'Certainly I attended it. But as I'd only just berthed here, and had to get hold of the right clothes, I was a bit late for the occasion.'

'I see. Then you came straight back here?'

'Obviously I did. I don't like fuss. I've been lying low.'

'That's something that appears to run in your family. And so, very decidedly, does something else.'

'May I ask what that is?' Adrian was now eyeing Appleby narrowly.

'A rash fondness for ingenious but really quite vulnerable lies. Mr Brockbank, your brother Christopher, having somehow got wind of your arrival here at Budleigh, came down yesterday evening and—I don't doubt—rowed out to see you just as I have done. It was something quite out of the blue. I don't know where you've come from, but you certainly haven't been receiving English news on the way. And here, suddenly, was your brother, chock-full of the craziest and most discreditable of his practical jokes. He'd resolved to attend his own memorial service, partly for the sheer hell of it, and partly to dramatize what he considered some loophole in the law. He'd plotted the thing ingeniously enough, and it had involved his impersonating you at the scene of an air-crash. He told you all this in exuberant detail. *You* had been made to appear the joker—this was the best part of *his* joke—and as a result of it he was officially dead until he chose to come alive again.' Appleby paused. 'Mr Brockbank,' he went on quietly, 'you decided that he never *would* so choose.'

'This is the most outrageous—'

'Please don't interrupt. What you said to yourself was this : if Christopher wanted to be dead, let him damned well *be* dead—and let his large fortune pass to his next of kin, yourself. It was all so simple, was it not ? Lie One : *you* had sworn to what was in fact the *true* identity of the dead man. Lie Two : *you* had been just in time for the memorial service. Your story would be simple and plausible. The true story, supposing anybody should tumble to it, would be too fantastic for credence. Have I succeeded in stating the matter with some succinctness ?'

'You have a kind of professional glibness, Sir John.' Adrian said this perfectly coolly. 'I suppose that for most of your days you've been ingeniously fudging up yarns like this. But it won't wash, you know. It won't wash, at all. You are reckoning that, at every step, it will be possible to collect one or another scrap of circumstantial evidence against me, and that these will just add up. But they won't—not to anything like the total that would persuade a jury of such nonsense. My poor brother met an accidental death in France, and I identified his body, and that's that.'

'On the contrary, your brother was murdered by you on this yacht yesterday evening; doubtless sewn up in canvas with as much in the way of miscellaneous metal objects as you could find on board; and sent over the side—far out at sea—last night.'

'Far out at sea ?' It was ironically that Adrian repeated

the words. 'Awkward, that. A body is rather a useful exhibit, is it not, when a thin case has to be proved?'

'Mr Brockbank, you entirely mistake the matter. There is absolute proof that your brother Christopher, alive and well, attended his own memorial service. It is a proof which, I know, he proposed to withhold from you for a time—which was perhaps a pity. But the evidence, which I need not particularize, is in my possession.'

'Dear me!' Adrian made a casual gesture which some-how didn't match with a suddenly alert look and a tautened frame. 'And is it in the possession of anybody else?'

'Yes, of several people. Otherwise, I'm bound to say I shouldn't be thus alone with you, Mr Brockbank, in a secluded situation. But it hadn't, I repeat, been evidence in *your* possession. For it wasn't in your brother's mind to mention its existence to you just at present. He was keeping it up *his* sleeve in case you proved to have something further up *your* sleeve. Rather a muzzy notion, perhaps, but under-standable when Brockbank is sparring with Brockbank. It is evidence, incidentally, which was entirely and ingeniously devised by your brother himself.' Appleby paused. 'I may just say that fingerprints come into it. Irrefutable things.'

There was a long silence, and then Adrian Brockbank, who had also been perched on a gunwale, stood up.

'If I may just slip below for a moment,' he said, 'I think I can turn up something which will put a term to this whole absurd affair.'

'As you please.'

It was only after a pause that Appleby had spoken. He might have been staring with interest at some small smudge of smoke on the horizon. For a couple of long minutes he continued immobile, sombrely waiting. For a further minute he continued so—even after the revolver shot had made itself heard. Then he rose with a small sigh and sought the late Adrian Brockbank below.

Appleby's Holidays

TWO ON A TOWER

I T   W A S   S O M E   years since the Barbacks had been abroad, and they decided to go to Italy. Or rather, Irene Barback decided this, and for once she carried her point. Charles whose responses to life were turning elderly far more quickly than they should, at first produced a surly opposition. He wasn't, he said, going to be pushed; and he continued for some time to collect and study illustrated brochures about a number of quite perversely dreary English seaside resorts. Then Irene had the bright idea of sending him to old Cheall, their family doctor.

Charles did, in fact, look rather badly run down, and anything about his health worried him tremendously. So the situation was hopeful, if only dear old Cheall could be persuaded to declare—whether with his tongue in his cheek or not—that Italy was quite definitely the tonic Charles required.

Irene remembered that all sorts of distinguished people had gone to Italy on medical advice—particularly poets, like Mrs Browning and John Keats. Her husband wasn't a poet—but he was a publisher, which is roughly the same sort of thing : and she felt that medicine and literature between them might get Charles on the move.

And they did. Old Cheall rang up and said rather bleakly that Charles would benefit from plenty of sunlight and plenty of distraction; and when Irene mentioned Italy Cheall replied that Italy would be just right. Then there was another piece of luck. Gregory Fan, Charles's junior partner, announced that he was motoring to Naples, and that it would be most delightful if the Barbacks joined up with him at least as far as Rome. Irene thought this quite wonder-ful—she had never hoped for such good fortune—and Charles kindled to the idea when it became clear that he wouldn't be asked to share the expenses of running Fan's car.

These were the circumstances in which the Barbacks set out for a country which the English have always tended to associate with violent passions and dark crimes.

Sir John Appleby encountered them in Florence. He wasn't there on holiday himself; he had gone over to con-sult with the police about security problems attending an international conference soon to be held in that hospitable city. But he had a few days at his disposal when these duties were finished, and he ran into Fan and his friends during a leisurely afternoon in the Uffizi.

He knew Gregory Fan as a man of considerable drive in more directions than one, and he was interested in the contrast between this restless personality and his very con-servative senior partner. Barback was senior in every sense, and certainly a good twenty years older than his wife. He didn't look a happy man. Nor, for that matter, did Irene Barback look a happy woman, although she was undoubtedly a strikingly beautiful one. Or *did* she look a happy woman, at least in some short-term way? The more settled lines on her face suggested boredom and frustration. But there was something else—something that you could get at only by noticing that she was making a very quiet and unobtrusive affair of her Italian holiday. She didn't have much to say to Fan. Indeed, she hardly looked at him. But there were some paintings in the Uffizi—not Florentine paintings, but glowing Venetian things, pulsing with sensuous life—that she seemed very well able to pass the time of day with.

'Did you hurry through to Italy?' Appleby asked. 'I usually find myself doing that.'

'Oh, no.' Fan had shaken his head. 'We've loitered along,

and lingered in all sorts of pleasant places. Haven't we, Charles?'

Charles Barback agreed. But, Appleby thought, it was in an oddly bewildered way, as if much in this holiday were a puzzle to him.

'And we intend to potter about a good deal here, too,' Fan said. 'What about coming with us to Monterino tomorrow?'

And Charles Barback, who had been staring rather sightlessly at a Carpaccio, turned round.

'Yes, do,' he said.

They made the trip in Fan's car, accompanied by Appleby's friend Cervoni, of the Ministry of Security. It was a wonderful day, and they stopped for a picnic lunch. Barback seemed depressed and reluctant to get on the road again. He fussed over the packing up; there was a wine-glass missing, and the cork wouldn't go back into the Chianti flask. He was almost certainly, Appleby thought, a tiresome man about the house. His wife, however, seemed scarcely to notice him. And at length they got on their way.

Monterino is an astonishing place; it stands on a hill, and in the Middle Ages its leading citizens vied with one another in building themselves tremendous towers. A sufficient number of these remain to suggest a sort of thirteenth-century first-cousin to Manhattan. You can climb some of these venerable skyscrapers and enjoy the most extensive views.

They climbed the tallest of the towers, and admired equally the tumble of picturesque roofs crowded immediately beneath them and the prospect of half Tuscany which lay beyond. Descending, they crossed the Piazza del Duomo towards a café where Irene Barback proposed they should explore the possibility of obtaining tea. But her husband and Fan became detached from the others, and when they looked back they saw the two men standing before another of the towers and waving to them.

'The Torre della Cisterna,' Cervoni explained politely. 'Our friends propose the ascent. But they signal, I think, that we should go forward and order our refreshment.'

So they went on to the café and sat down. It was in a corner of the square from which the Torre della Cisterna was clearly visible.

And thus, five minutes later, they all three saw the thing happen. What drew their attention to the top of the tower was a scream—and an instant later they realised that it was Barback's voice. The scream came again—it was a high-pitched desperate call for help—and then they saw Barback himself appear from behind a turret and stagger backwards. He was clutching his face; suddenly he thrust out his arms as if to avoid a blow; and then he ran forward as if making a dash for safety. The movement took him once more out of sight. There was another scream; then silence; then a hubbub of many voices calling from the other side of the tower.

Appleby was already up and running; presently he was thrusting his way through a horrified little crowd: some of them tourists, most of them inhabitants of Monterino. They formed a ragged circle round what was all too clearly Charles Barback's dead body. It lay, dreadfully crushed and gashed, in the hot Italian dust—having fallen first to one roof and then to another, much as a ball might helplessly do on a pin-table.

Appleby turned away, rounded a corner, and arrived before the entrance of the tower just as Gregory Fan staggered out of it. Fan's hands were thrust deep in his pockets.

'I wasn't . . .' he stammered. 'I didn't . . . I couldn't . . .'

Without speaking, Appleby pointed. And then—slowly, helplessly—Fan brought his hands from their concealment and held them out. They were covered with blood.

*　　*　　*

'Certainly Barback's blood.' Appleby, sitting in the Palazzo Municipale and beginning explanations to Cervoni, was in a very dusty state. He had been clambering hazardously over the rooftops of Monterino; and now on the table before him were a pen-knife and some small fragments of thin, curved glass. 'It was probably a good idea, declaring at our picnic that a wine-glass was missing; if he hadn't, and its disappearance had been noticed later, one of us might have begun wondering.'

'He needed a receptacle?'

'Precisely. He slashed his wrist, collected the blood, and then put on that turn for the benefit of people on the ground below. At the first scream, Fan must have gone running up from the final chamber of the tower—a sort of museum—where he had been lingering. You can imagine him wondering what on earth had happened.'

'My dear Sir John—indeed, yes.'

'As he opened the door giving access to the roof, Barback tipped the blood on him, slashed himself again for good measure, gave another scream, hurled the wine-glass and pocketknife as far as he could across the rooftops of Monterino, and pitched himself over the parapet.'

'Revenge?'

'Just that. He knew of the intrigue that was going on between his wife and Fan. And from what your doctor says, it is clear he must have known that he was mortally ill. He didn't mind dying a little sooner, if he could leave the suggestion that his wife's lover had attacked him with fatal consequences on the Torre della Cisterna.' Appleby turned to Irene Barback, who was sitting immobile in a corner of the room. 'I'm sorry. But it is best that you should understand the whole thing at once.'

The wretched woman nodded. She appeared quite dazed.

'Charles wouldn't be pushed,' she whispered strangely. 'But he would jump.'

BEGGAR WITH SKULL

A motor tour in the West Country makes it possible to visit any number of historic houses. Having done Montacute that morning, and being pledged to do Barrington Court in the afternoon, Sir John Appleby rather hoped to slip past Roydon Abbey without stopping. But his wife would have nothing of this.

'There's a famous El Greco,' she said. 'Turn in.'

They turned in. Lord Roydon's country seat was imposing but not exactly flourishing. The house could have done with a lick of paint, and the grounds with a few more gardeners. Perhaps his lordship was something of an absentee. Certainly there was no flag flying, so presumably he wasn't lurking about now. But this made it only the more certain that the Applebys would be allowed to look round. Appleby foresaw another long tramp through a succession of chilly splendours. But his wife was adamant. She closed the guide-book she had been consulting.

'There's nothing about it being open to the public,' she said. 'So you'd better see if you've got a pound note.'

'Quite so.' Appleby was resigned. 'You said an El Greco?'

'Yes. The Beggar with Skull.'

'Good Lord!' Appleby was impressed. 'I couldn't call a pound absolutely outrageous if I'm going to see that.'

They were received by the housekeeper, a myopic old person who appeared well used to the job. She stood them in the middle of a vast panelled hall and began a lecture.

'The family is of great antiquity,' she said. 'Doutremeres

have lived on this spot for more than nine hundred years. But his lordship is not in residence just at present.'

Appleby reflected that this break with tradition was a pity. But Judith Appleby seemed possessed of some relevant information.

'Isn't Lord Roydon a great yachtsman?' she prompted.

The old housekeeper beamed. The present Marquis was certainly much distinguished in that line.

'Of course,' she purred, 'his lordship has the magnificent physique of all the Doutremeres. It's in the blood, I say. And there is his portrait. Presented by the tenantry on the occasion of his lordship's giving up active command.'

Appleby and Judith looked with due respect at the portrait. Lord Roydon had a red face and a red beard, and he had been painted against a red sky in what appeared to be the uniform of a Vice-admiral of the Fleet. As the artist had somehow contrived to indicate that his subject wasn't much short of seven feet tall the effect was altogether impressive.

'And next to him is his brother Lord Charles Doutremere.'

With suitably modified awe, the Applebys looked at this portrait too. Lord Charles was another giant. He was depicted, sideways-on, as clean-shaven, florid, and in garments appropriate to shooting things. He looked, indeed, quite as if he would shoot anything on sight. A red setter was eyeing him apprehensively from the bottom left-hand corner.

'His lordship—' the housekeeper began, and then broke off. 'But here he is,' she added in a lower voice, and in some confusion. 'He's got back.'

It was certainly true. Lord Roydon, in untidy nautical kit, strode through the screen at the bottom of the hall. Seeing the Applebys, he gave a brisk bow, barked out a 'Good afternoon', and marched on. Which was civility enough, Appleby reflected. Then suddenly Lord Roydon stopped dead in his tracks and pointed at an empty space on the wall.

'Mrs Cumpsty,' he snapped, 'what's become of the El Greco?'

'The El Greco, my lord? Why, it hasn't come back since you took it away.'

'Since I took it away! What the devil are you talking about?'

Mrs Cumpsty stared.

'Why, three weeks ago, my lord. The last time you called in. You had a word with me here in the hall, my lord. And then you took away the picture—' Mrs Cumpsty faltered, as she well might in face of the enraged appearance of her employer. 'And then you took away the picture, saying you were going to have it cleaned in London.'

'Absolute nonsense! You're mad, Mrs Cumpsty—or in collusion with some scoundrelly thief. I haven't been near the Abbey for six weeks.'

Mrs Cumpsty—very naturally—began to weep. And Sir John Appleby stepped forward and introduced himself. It was clearly going to be a case for the police.

The housekeeper stuck to her story. She was quite certain that it had been Lord Roydon himself who had taken away El Greco's Beggar with Skull. His lordship had been most affable and had chatted about various Abbey affairs in a manner that no imposter could have managed. If there had been the slightest cause for suspicion she certainly wouldn't have let the picture go.

Appleby inquired whether anybody else had been aware of Lord Roydon's—or the supposed Lord Roydon's visit. The whole household had of course heard of it. But only one of the Abbey's two footmen had actually set eyes on him—having admitted him in the first place and then been sent to summon Mrs Cumpsty. This young man also was certain that it had been Lord Roydon.

'Anybody else? Can you think, sir, of anybody else we ought to see?' asked Appleby.

Lord Roydon considered for a moment.

'The children,' he barked. 'Half a dozen about the place. Gardeners' kids, and so forth. Sharp nippers.'

It seemed an astute suggestion—and it bore astonishing fruit. The fourth child interviewed was a small boy called Alf. Alf confessed, amid tears and surprising terror, that he had indeed seen Lord Roydon. He had seen him while playing near a little-frequented cart-track through the park. His lordship had been preparing to drive away in an unfamiliar car. Alf appeared to brace himself at this point in his narrative.

'But first, sir, 'e stopped and took 'is beard off.'

'Dear me!' Appleby said mildly. 'Did you ever see his lordship do that before, Alf?'

'No, sir,' Alf gulped. 'But then 'e saw me a-watching, sir. And 'e came after me and said e'd break my jaw if ever I told on 'im.'

'Now, Alf, this was clearly a man wearing a *false* beard. So could it have been his lordship?'

'No, sir.'

'And are you sure that you have never seen this man before?'

Alf was confident.

'No, sir. But I'd know 'im again. I'd know 'im by his size, and by a great scar on his chin.'

'That will do!' Surprisingly, Lord Roydon seized the small boy and ran him out of the hall. Then he turned to Appleby. 'The matter is not to be pursued,' he said shortly. 'Be good enough to consider it closed.'

But Appleby had turned to the portrait of Lord Roydon's brother, Lord Charles Doutremere—the portrait painted in profile.

'I think not,' he said grimly.

Lord Charles was indeed a more than typical Doutremere recluse. He lived in a remote cottage some twenty miles away, attended by only a single manservant. And the man, although respectful to Lord Roydon, was reluctant to admit them.

'Lord Charles's condition is still critical,' he said. 'The doctor advises there should be no visitors, my lord.'

And Lord Roydon turned pale.

'Critical? What the devil do you mean?'

'A hunting accident a month ago, my lord. Lord Charles insisted you shouldn't be let know. He spoke'—the man hesitated—'he spoke of the bad blood between you, my lord.'

Appleby gave Lord Roydon a single glance, and then turned again to the man.

'Just what sort of accident?'

'To the spine, sir. Lord Charles hasn't been able to stir from his bed for over a month.'

It was a couple of hours later, and the Applebys were on their way to inspect Barrington Court—much as if nothing had happened.

'I still don't really understand,' Judith Appleby said.

'Lord Roydon's determination was to sell his El Greco secretly, and at the same time to collect insurance on it. That meant, of course, finding a collector content to keep the thing more or less permanently hidden away. But, as you know, a few such odd chaps, rolling in the necessary money, do exist.'

'Arrested development, or something.'

'No doubt. Well, our friend Lord Roydon shaved. He painted a scar on his jaw. He put on a false beard and interviewed Mrs Cumpsty. It's not surprising the short-sighted old soul was so sure it *was* Lord Roydon, since a beard would be a beard to her, whether false or authentic. Then, having made off with the picture, his lordship went through that pantomime with poor young Alf. No wonder he had that inspiration about my questioning the children.'

'You mean—'

'Yes—he was planning to plant the theft very ingeniously on his brother. Not at all pretty, but there it was. And the plan broke down only because of that hunting accident, which was bound to give the unfortunate Charles an absolute alibi. Only Lord Roydon—as we heard—had learnt nothing about that, since the brothers very seldom communicated with each other.'

'But if Lord Roydon *shaved* his beard—'

'He simply went off in his yacht and waited for it to grow. And then he turned up at the Abbey again—a few minutes after we did.' Appleby paused, and when he spoke again there was a note of professional admiration in his voice. 'Really quite a remarkable criminal formula. Unique, I imagine. X disguised as Y disguised as X. Think it out like that.'

Appleby glanced at his watch, accelerated, and laughed softly.

'One has to call it,' he said, 'a notably bare-faced fraud.'

THE EXPLODING BATTLESHIP

S ITTING IN FRONT of Florian's café in Venice, Lady Appleby counted her resources. She began with her remaining traveller's cheques, went on to Italian bank-notes, and ended up with small-change. Her husband divided his attention between watching this operation tolerantly—Judith was always extremely businesslike on holidays—and surveying the tourists who thronged the Piazza San Marco.

It was the height of the season. There were Germans fathoms deep in guide books, Americans obsessively intent on peering into cameras, and English with their brows furrowed in various degrees of that financial anxiety which Judith herself was evincing. There were also some Italians. These, Appleby thought, appeared agreeably carefree.

'And six days to go,' Judith said. She had arrived at her grand total. 'Of course, we have to remember the children's presents. I've got a list.' She produced a notebook. 'A mechanical mouse that squeaks and runs; a hunting-crop that turns into a stiletto; an exploding battleship; an atomic submarine; a bone or some other bit of an old saint or martyr; and three caskets in gold, silver, and lead.'

'I'm surprised,' Appleby said, 'that Bobby didn't add an heiress: Portia as well as her caskets. "In Belmont is a lady richly left." It sounds most attractive. But don't you think they all sound rather unlikely objects to pick up in Venice? Even the lethal hunting-crop.'

'Pardon me.' A polite American voice sounded in the Appleby's ears. 'But I guess I'd like to know what is meant by an exploding battleship.'

*   *   *

The American was at the next table. He was elderly and had the air of feeling lonesome. He was also—Appleby decided with his policeman's habit of rapid appraisal—wealthy, unsophisticated, and highly intelligent.

'An exploding battleship?' Appleby turned his chair round and addressed the stranger companionably. 'It's built up, I think, in a number of interlocking sections, and there's some sort of simple spring-mechanism inside. You shoot at it with a little gun. And when you hit the vital spot, the spring is released, and the whole thing flies into bits.'

'Sure.' The American produced this monosyllable thoughtfully and with much deliberation. Then he turned to Judith. 'Marm,' he said courteously, 'I can direct you to that mechanical mouse. The small toy-store at this end of the Merceria dell' Orologio.' He paused, and then addressed Appleby. 'Would you be in the way, sir, of buying objects of antique art in this remarkable town?'

'Well, no.' Appleby was amused by this question. 'I used to pick up very modest things here once upon a time. But I don't nowadays.'

The stranger nodded wisely.

'In that case,' he said, 'I needn't communicate to you a certain darned nasty suspicion building up in my mind right now.'

And with this cryptic remark the elderly American stood up, made Judith Appleby a careful bow, and walked away.

Four days later Appleby received an unexpected request to call on the Chief of Police. He made his way in some perplexity to the Fondamenta San Lorenzo, and was received with great politeness.

'My dear Sir John,' the functionary said, 'it was decided by one of my officers that you must be questioned. But when I discovered in you a distinguished colleague, I ventured to give myself the pleasure of inviting you to call. You were well acquainted with Mr Conklin?'

'Conklin?' Appleby was perplexed.

'An American visitor with whom one of our *vigili* happened to observe you in conversation in the Piazza on Monday.' The Chief of Police spread out his hands expressively. 'A most elusive and unobtrusive man. He proved to be unaccompanied by a wife or other companion. We can discover almost nothing about him, so far. Except, indeed, that the gentleman was a millionaire.'

'*Was?*' Appleby said.

'Alas, yes. His body has been recovered from the lagoon. And almost certainly there has been foul play. A perplexing affair. We do not like unresolved mysteries in Venice.'

'Nor do we care for them in London, my dear sir. But what you tell me is most surprising. Mr Conklin seemed a most inoffensive man, quite unlikely to get into trouble.' Appleby reflected for a moment. 'You know *nothing* about him?'

'It appears that he was something of an art-collector. Not, perhaps, among the more highly-informed in the field. But—as I have said—a millionaire.'

'In other words, a ready-made dupe?'

'It is sad, Sir John.' The Chief of Police again made his expressive gesture. 'But they have much wealth, these people. And they come among us, who have little wealth, but much colourable junk lying ready to our hand. I command very poor English, I fear. But at least I make myself comprehensible?'

'Certainly you do. And you feel, I think, that drowning the dupes is going rather too far?'

'It is my sentiment in the matter. Decidedly.'

Again Appleby reflected.

'My encounter with this unfortunate man,' he said, 'was of the slightest, as I shall explain. But I believe I can possibly help you, all the same.'

'My dear Sir John, I am enchanted.'

'Only I am afraid it may cost money. Or at least *look* as if it were costing money.'

'*Non importa*,' the Chief of Police said.

Appleby began by buying—or appearing to buy—a genuine Tintoretto. He followed this up with a clamantly spurious Carpaccio, and then with a Guardi so authentically lovely that he could hardly bear to reflect on how fictitious his purchase really was. Judith sometimes watched him covertly from over the way. It intrigued her to think that she might really have married an American precisely like this.

It was on the third day that Appleby made the acquaintance of the Conte Alfonso Forobosco. This gentleman's conversation, casually offered over a *cappuccino*, showed him to be familiarly acquainted not only with his fellow members of the Italian aristocracy but also with the President of the Republic, the exiled Royal Family, and most of the more important dignitaries in the Vatican. All of which didn't prevent Conte Alfonso from being hard up. This fact, emerging in due season and with delightful candour, precluded the further revelation that he was even constrained, from time to time, to part with a few of the innumerable artistic treasures which had descended to him from his ancestors.

All this was extremely impressive. And so was the speed with which the Conte worked. Half an hour later, Appleby found himself in a gaunt and semi-derelict *palazzo* on the Grand Canal.

'The goblets,' Conte Alfonso said, 'belonged to Machiavelli. The pistols were Mazzini's. The writing-table was used by Manzoni.'

Appleby made the sort of responses he judged appropriate in a wealthy American. The *palazzo*—or its *piano nobile* at least—had been well stocked with a variety of imposing objects. And presently the Conte came to the most imposing of the lot : a species of elaborately convoluted urn in Venetian glass. Appleby doubted whether anything more completely hideous had ever issued from the glass-factories on Murano.

'The poison-vase of Lucrezia Borgia,' the Conte said, pointing to it on a table. 'Take it—but carefully—and hold it up to the light.'

Appleby did as he was told. But even as he raised the precious object in his two hands there was an ominous crack. And then he was looking at its shattered fragments lying at his feet.

Conte Alfonso gave an agonised cry. Then, with a gesture magnificently magnanimous, he stopped, picked up the pieces, strode to a window, and pitched them into the Grand Canal of Venice.

'*Non fa niente*,' he said. 'No matter. An accident. And you are my guest.'

Appleby went through a pantomime of extreme contrition and dismay. The least he could do, he intimated, was to pay up. The Conte protested. Appleby insisted. Reluctantly the Conte named a sum—a nominal sum, a bare million lire. And then Appleby led him to the window.

'At least,' he said, 'I may get back the bits.'

And this seemed true. Several police launches were diverting the *vaporetti* and other traffic on the canal. Just beneath the window a frogman was already at work. It would have been possible to reflect that there was an authentic Carpaccio depicting a very similar scene.

'And now I think you have visitors,' Appleby said, turning round. 'Including your Chief of Police himself.'

'It was this so-called Conte Alfonso's regular racket?' Judith asked afterwards.

'Certainly it was.' Appleby paused in the task of packing his suitcase. 'The fellow had a steady supply of Lucrezia Borgia's tea-pots, or whatever. Two seconds after you picked them up, the spring went off and shattered them. And then, of course, the problem was to get rid of the evidence. But there lay the advantage of having the scene of the operation on the Grand Canal. The Conte made detection impossible simply by putting on that aristocratic turn of gathering up the bits and chucking them into the water. Our friend Conklin, however, was a shrewd chap in his way, and he suspected he'd been had. When I explained about the exploding battleship, the full truth flashed on him.'

'So he went back and taxed the Conte with the fraud?'

'Just that. And the scoundrel—rather an engaging scoundrel if he hadn't gone so decidedly too far—liquidated him at once. Quite in the antique Venetian manner, I suppose one may say. But, apart from that, there was certainly nothing genuinely antique about him.'

A knock came at the bedroom door, and a hotel servant handed in a parcel. Appleby received it, regarded it doubtfully, and then opened it up. What lay inside was the little Guardi.

'John!'—Judith was very startled—'you haven't really gone and bought the thing?'

'Of course not.' Appleby had opened a letter. 'It's a present—call it from the Doge and the Serenissimi.'

'Meaning from the mayor and city council?'

'That does make it sound a good deal more prosaic. But remember for how long Venice held the gorgeous East in fee. She seems capable of decidedly regal behaviour still.'

THE BODY IN THE GLEN

'Dr Watson,' Appleby said, 'once discovered
with some surprise that his friend Sherlock Holmes was uncommonly vague about the workings of the Solar System.
Holmes explained that he hadn't much interest in acquiring
useless information—useless, that's to say, from his professional point of view, which was that of a dedicated enemy
of crime. But the truth is that some scrap of quite out-of-the-
way knowledge may turn out uncommonly useful to a
detective. For example, there was that Highland holiday of
ours. Judith, you remember that? It was when we stumbled
upon the mystery of Glen Mervie.'

'The affair that began with my refusing the milk?' Lady
Appleby said cryptically. 'It was most obtuse of me.'

I scented a story in this.

'I can't believe,' I murmured diplomatically, 'that Judith
would ever be obtuse. But just what happened?'

'My friend Ian Grant,' Appleby began, 'is Laird of
Mervie, and the place runs to some uncommonly good shooting in a small way—to say nothing of a trout stream that's
a perfect wonder. So I always enjoy a holiday there, and so
does Judith. But this particular holiday turned out to be of
the busman's sort. When, I mean, they found Andrew
Strachan's body lying by the Drochet.'

'Ah,' I said. 'Drenched in gore?'

'Certainly.'

'Capital, Appleby. Your reminiscences, if I may say so,
tend to be a little on the bloodless side. But here is a certain
Andrew Strachan steeped in the stuff. Proceed.'

'Actually, I'll go back a bit—at least to the previous day. Grant and I had been shooting over a neighbour's moor, and Judith came to join us in the afternoon. We drove back to Mervie together, and Grant stopped just outside the village to speak to one of his tenants, an old woman called Mrs Frazer. Mrs Frazer's sole possession seemed to be a cow, and she was milking it when we all went and had a word with her. She wasn't interested in me, but she looked at Judith rather searchingly. And then she offered her a drink of milk straight from the cow. Judith refused it. I think she felt that poor old Mrs Frazer needed whatever dairy produce she could raise, and oughtn't to be giving it away.'

'And that,' I asked, 'was what was obtuse? The old woman was offended that Judith declined her hospitality?'

'It wasn't quite that—as I realised when Grant stepped forward and insisted rather peremptorily that Judith should change her mind. He apologised later. It was a matter, it seemed, of the Evil Eye.'

'The Evil Eye!' I was startled.

'Just that. Didn't the poet Collins write an *Ode on the Popular Superstitions of the Highlands*? The Evil Eye is very much one of them. But, of course, you come on the idea all over Europe.'

'The Italians,' I said, 'call it the *Malocchio*.'

'Quite so. Well, Mrs Frazer had decided that Judith was perhaps the possessor of the Evil Eye. It's widely believed to accompany great physical beauty.' Appleby paused happily on this obvious invention. 'Anyway, the point seemed to be this: Mrs Frazer's cow would die unless the magic was defeated. There are various ways of defeating the Evil Eye, and the surest of them is obliging its possessor to accept a gift. Hence the milk.'

'Superstition of that sort is still widely prevalent in those parts?'

'Most certainly. Grant talked to us very interestingly on

the subject that evening. He had a shepherd some way up Glen Mervie whose possession of the Evil Eye was one of the terrors of the region. And there's great belief, too, in various forms of Second Sight—particularly in what's known as Calling—and in family apparitions and so forth. Ian Grant himself would be regarded as no true Laird of Mervie if he admitted that he hadn't in fact seen the spectre of a white horse on the night his father died on the battle-field.'

'And Andrew Strachan,' I asked, 'whose body was found by the Drochet? I suppose the Drochet is a burn?'

'Yes. It rises on Ben Cailie, and runs through the Glen of Mervie to join the Garry. As for Andrew Strachan, I took him to be one of Grant's tenants. But actually he wasn't. His father had been a crofter who bought his own farm. So Andrew Strachan was a landowner himself in a very small way—which was what enabled him to keep his younger brother Donald so harshly under his thumb. If Donald had been a tenant of Grant's he'd have had a square deal. As it was, he worked for his brother Andrew, who was a very hard man. They lived in neighbouring cottages in a clachan a mile beyond the village, which is itself a pretty remote spot. There was only their mother—and she was over eighty—who heard a word of their quarrel.'

'Ought you to tell me they'd had a quarrel? Isn't it giving too much away?'

'You'll find out in a minute. In any case, they *did* have a tremendous quarrel—on that very afternoon, as it happened, that Mrs Frazer gave Judith the milk.

'Donald Strachan's story of what followed was quite simple. The quarrel came to nothing, and later that evening Andrew set off up the glen for Dunwinnie. He was courting there. Or rather, if Donald was to be believed, he was after a woman there who was no better than she should be. It was the sad fact, Donald said, that his brother would often spend half the night in Dunwinnie, drinking a great deal with this ungodly wench, and then he'd come stealing home before daybreak. Such goings-on, you understand, have to be conducted much on the quiet in that part of the world. The kirk and the minister are still powers in the land.'

'And I suppose Donald's suggestion was that Andrew had simply met with an accident?'

'Just that. And all the facts—or nearly all the facts— were such as to make it quite possible. There's a point half-way down the glen where the path forks. One branch climbs imperceptibly, and eventually skirts the verge of some very high rocks overhanging the burn. It was at the foot of these that Andrew Strachan's body was found. His skull was cracked open, and in a way that was a quite conceivable consequence of a perfectly possible fall.'

'In all probability,' Appleby went on, 'there would have been no serious question about what had happened, if it hadn't been for one very queer thing. The lad who found Andrew Strachan dead found Donald Strachan, too—alive and not a couple of hundred yards away. Donald had fractured a thigh, as a man might do who had a bad fall while running blindly among rocks. It seemed a queer coincidence that both brothers should meet with an accident on the same night. And what was Donald doing in the glen, anyway? He had an explanation to offer. It was an uncommonly odd one.'

Appleby paused for a moment. He is rather a practiced retailer of yarns of this sort.

'I mentioned what, in the Highlands, they term Calling. It's supposed that, in some supernatural way, a man may sometimes hear his own name being called out by a relation, or a friend, who at that moment is either dying or in great danger in what may be some quite distant spot. It might be Canada, for example, or Australia.'

'I've heard of it,' I said. 'Indeed, isn't it on record as rather well-attested?'

'Yes, it is—although I don't know what a court of law

would make of it. And it looked as if a court of law would have to try. Because Donald Strachan's story was simply that, in the middle of the night, and after their abortive quarrel, he had heard Andrew *calling*. He said he somehow knew at once that it was a *calling* in this rather special sense. And as he was aware that Andrew had gone up the glen to Dunwinnie, he got up and made his way there himself, convinced that there had been an accident or a fatality. And he hurried so recklessly through the darkness that he had his own utterly disabling fall.'

I digested all this for a moment in silence.

'It would certainly have been a hard nut for a judge and jury,' I said. 'But what did you think yourself?'

'I saw another possibility. It wasn't pretty, but at least it had the merit of *not* involving the supernatural. Donald, I supposed, had crept into Andrew's cottage in the night, battered him to death, and then lugged the body to the one spot in the neighbourhood where the appearance of a fatal accident could be made credible. And he'd never have been suspected if he hadn't had his own tumble among the rocks.'

'But had you any evidence?'

'There *was* one piece of evidence.' Appleby paused again. 'And it was I,' he went on rather drily, 'who pointed it out to the local police. The Strachans were both wretchedly poor, and their clothes were little better than rags. And that did rather obscure what was nevertheless clear when one looked hard enough. Andrew's body was fully dressed. But his jacket was on inside out.'

'So you concluded—?'

'I concluded that his body had been shoved into it, and probably into the rest of his clothes, in the dark.'

'It was certainly a fair inference. In fact, my dear Appleby, I can't think of any other explanation.'

'Ah—but remember the Solar System. Holmes *might* conceivably have been caught out by his ignorance of it. And I was being caught out by—well, by my ignorance of those popular superstitions of the Highlands. You remember my telling you that up that glen there was a shepherd whose possession of the Evil Eye was a terror to the district?'

'Certainly I do.'

'Well, it seems there are more ways of averting the Evil Eye than by offering a drink of milk. You can avert it—at least from harming your own person—simply by wearing any of your garments inside out.'

'Widdershins!'

'Yes, indeed—that's the general name for such behaviour. And nobody up there would dream of going through the Glen of Mervie without taking that precaution. So you see the police—and my host, for that matter—distinctly had the laugh on me.'

'It was no laughing matter.'

'That's true. But there was clearly no case against Donald Strachan. He just had to be believed.'

DEATH IN THE SUN

THE VILLA STOOD on a remote Cornish cape. Its flat roof commanded a magnificent view, but was not itself commanded from anywhere. So it was a good spot either for sun-bathing, or for suicide of a civilised and untroublesome sort. George Elwin appeared to have put it to both uses successively. His dead body lay on the roof, bronzed and stark naked—or stark naked except for a wrist watch. The gun lay beside him. His face was a mess.

'I don't usually bring my week-end guests to view this kind of thing.' The Chief Constable had glanced in honest apology at Appleby. 'But you're a professional, after all.'

'Fair enough.' Appleby gazed down dispassionately at the corpse. 'What kind of a chap was this Elwin?'

'Wealthy, for a start. But—as you can see—retaining some unassuming tastes.' The Chief Constable had pointed to the watch, which was an expensive one, but on a simple leather strap. 'Poor devil!' he added softly. 'Think, Appleby, of taking a revolver and doing that to yourself.'

'Mayn't somebody have murdered him? A thief? This is an out-of-the-way place, and you say he lived here in solitude, working on his financial schemes, for weeks at a time. Anybody might come and go.'

'True enough. But there's £5,000 in notes in a drawer downstairs. An unlocked drawer, heaven help us! And Elwin's fingerprints are on the gun—the fellow I sent along this morning established that. So there's no mystery, I'm afraid. And another thing: George Elwin had a history.'

'You mean, he'd tried to kill himself before?'

'Just that. He was a hypochondriac, and always taking

drugs. And he suffered from periodic fits of melancholy. Last year, it seems, he took an enormous dose of barbiturate—and was discovered just in time, naked like this in a lonely cove. He seems to have had a fancy for death in the sun.'

'I think I'd prefer it to death in the dark.' As he said this, Appleby knelt beside the body. Gently, he turned over the left hand and removed the wrist watch. It was still going. On its back the initials *G. E.* were engraved in the gold. Equally gently, Appleby returned the watch to the wrist, and buckled the strap. For a moment he paused, frowning.

'Do you know,' he said, 'I'd rather like to have a look at his bedroom.'

The bedroom confirmed the impression made by the watch. The furnishings were simple, but the simplicity was of the kind that costs money. Appleby opened a wardrobe and looked at the clothes. He removed a couple of suits and studied them with care. He returned one, and laid the other on the bed.

'Just what did you mean,' he asked, 'by saying that Elwin was always taking drugs?'

'Ambiguous expression nowadays, I agree. He kept doctoring himself—messing around with medicines. Just take a glance into that corner-cupboard. Regular chemist's shop.'

The cupboard was certainly crammed with medicine bottles and pill boxes. Appleby took rather more than a glance. He started a systematic examination.

'Proprietary stuffs,' he said. 'But they mostly carry their pharmaceutical name as well. What's tetracycline for, would you suppose? Ah, it's an antibiotic. The poor chap was afraid of infections. Do you know? You could work out all his fears and phobias from this cupboard.'

'A curious thought,' the Chief Constable said grimly.

'Various antihistamines—no doubt he went in for allergies in a big way. Benzocaine, dexamphetamine, sulphafurazole —terrible mouthfuls they are.'

'In every sense, I'd suppose.'

'Quite so. A suntan preparation. But look, barbiturates again. He could have gone out that way if he'd wanted to. There's enough to kill an elephant, and Elwin's not all that bulky. Endless analgesics. You can bet he was always expecting pain.' Appleby closed the cupboard door, and glanced round the rest of the room. 'By the way, how do you propose to have the body identified at the inquest?'

'Identified?' The Chief Constable stared.

'Just a thought. His dentist, perhaps?'

'As a matter of fact, that wouldn't work. The police surgeon examined his mouth this morning. Teeth perfect— Elwin probably hadn't been to a dentist since he was a child. But, of course, the matter's merely formal, since there can't be any doubt of his identity. I didn't know him well, but I recognize him myself, more or less—even with his face like that.'

'I see. By the way, how does one bury a naked corpse? Still naked? It seems disrespectful. In a shroud? No longer fashionable. Perhaps just in a nice business suit.' Appleby turned to the bed. 'I think we'll dress George Elwin that way now.'

'My dear fellow!'

'Just rummage in those drawers, would you?' Appleby was inexorable. 'Underclothes and a shirt, but you needn't bother about socks or a tie.'

Ten minutes later the body, still supine on the roof, was almost fully clothed. The two men looked down at it sombrely.

'Yes,' the Chief Constable said slowly. 'I see what you had in mind.'

'I think we need some information about George Elwin's connections. And about his relatives, in particular. What do you know about that yourself?'

'Not much.' The Chief Constable took a restless turn up and down the flat room. 'He had a brother named Arnold

Elwin. Rather a bad-hat brother, or at least a shiftless one, living mostly in Canada, but turning up from time to time to cash in on his brother George's increasing wealth.'

'Arnold would be about the same age as George?'

'That's my impression. They may have been twins, for that matter.' The Chief Constable broke off. 'In heaven's name, Appleby, what put this hoary old piece of melodrama in your head?'

'Look at this.' Appleby was again kneeling by the body. Again he turned over the left hand so that the strap of the wrist watch was revealed. 'What do you see on the leather, a third of an inch outward from the present position of the buckle?'

'A depression.' The Chief Constable was precise. 'A narrow and discoloured depression, parallel with the line of the buckle itself.'

'Exactly. And what does that suggest?'

'That the watch really belongs to another man—someone with a slightly thicker wrist.'

'And those clothes, now that we've put them on the dead man?'

'Well, they remind me of something in *Macbeth*.' The Chief Constable smiled faintly. 'Something about a giant's robe on a dwarfish thief.'

'I'd call that poetic exaggeration. But the general picture is clear. It will be interesting to discover whether we have to go as far as Canada to come up with—'

Appleby broke off. The Chief Constable's chauffeur had appeared on the roof. He glanced askance at the body, and then spoke hastily.

'Excuse me, sir, but a gentleman has just driven up, asking for Mr Elwin. He says he's Mr Elwin's brother.'

'Thank you, Pengelly,' the Chief Constable said unemotionally. 'We'll come down.' But when the chauffeur had gone he turned to Appleby with a low whistle. 'Talk of the devil!' he said.

'Or, at least, of the villain in the hoary old melodrama?'
Appleby glanced briefly at the body. 'Well, let's go and see.'

As they entered the small study downstairs, a lanky figure
rose from a chair by the window. There could be no doubt
that the visitor looked remarkably like the dead man.

'My name is Arnold Elwin,' he said. 'I have called to see
my brother. May I ask—'

'Mr Elwin,' the Chief Constable said formally, 'I deeply
regret to inform you that your brother is dead. He was found
on the roof this morning, shot through the head.'

'Dead?' The lanky man sank into his chair again. 'I can't
believe it! Who are you?'

'I am the Chief Constable of the County, and this is my
guest Sir John Appleby, the Commissioner of Metropolitan
Police. He is very kindly assisting me in my inquiries—as
you, sir, may do. Did you see your brother yesterday?'

'Certainly. I had just arrived in England, and I came
straight here, as soon as I learned that George was going
in for one of his periodical turns as a recluse.'

'There was nobody else about the place when you made
this call?'

'Nobody. George managed for himself, except for a
woman who came in from the village early in the morning.
His manner of life was extremely eccentric. And solitude
was the very last thing that a man of his morbid temperament should have allowed himself.'

'It was a suicidal temperament?'

'Of course it was. And what point is there in dodging the
thing? George had made one attempt on his own life already.'

'That is true. May I ask whether you had—well, a satisfactory interview with him?'

'Nothing of the kind. George and I disagreed. So I said
good day to him, and cleared out.'

'Your disagreement would be about family affairs? Money
—that kind of thing?'

'I'm damned if I see what business it is of yours.'

There was a moment's silence, during which the Chief Constable appeared to brood darkly. Then he tried to catch Appleby's eye, but failed to do so. Finally he advanced firmly on the lanky man.

'George Elwin—' he began.

'What the deuce do you mean? My name, sir, as you very well know, is Arnold Elwin, not—'

'George Elwin, by virtue of my commission and office I arrest you in the Queen's name. You will be brought before the magistrate, and charged with the wilful murder of your brother, Arnold Elwin.'

Appleby had been prowling round the room, peering at the books, opening and shutting drawers. Now he came to a halt, and spoke with distinguishable caution.

'It may be irregular,' he said to the Chief Constable. 'But I think we might explain to Mr Elwin, as we can safely call him, just what is in our minds.'

'As you please, Appleby.' The Chief Constable was a shade stiff. 'But be good enough to do it yourself.'

Appleby nodded, and then spent a moment in thought.

'Mr Elwin,' he said gravely, 'it is within our knowledge that Mr George Elwin, the owner of this house, was, or is, subject to phases of acute melancholia. Last year, one of these attacks led him to an actual attempt at suicide—to which, indeed, you have just referred. That is our first fact.

'The second is this: the wrist watch found on the dead man's hand was not fastened as it would normally have been fastened on the wrist of its owner. The dead man's is a slimmer wrist.

'A third fact connects with the second. The clothes in this house are too big for the dead man.' Appleby paused. 'But the Chief Constable and I are obliged to reflect that they would fit you very well.'

'You're mad!' the lanky man got to his feet again. 'There's not a word of truth—'

'I can only give you what has been in our minds—emphasise the tentative nature of what I am advancing. Having said so much, I come to a fourth fact. George and Arnold Elwin were not readily distinguishable. You agree?'

'Of course I agree. George and I were twins.'

'Or Arnold and you were twins—for we must continue to bear an open mind. And now, what I shall call our hypothesis is as follows: you, George Elwin, living in solitude in this house, were visited by your brother Arnold, just back from Canada. He demanded money or the like, perhaps under some threat of damaging disclosure. There was a violent quarrel between you, and you shot him dead—at hideously close quarters.

'Now, sir, what could you do? The wound was compatible with suicide. But who would believe that Arnold had arrived here, gained possession of your gun, and shot himself?

'Fortunately there was somebody who *would* readily be believed to have committed suicide, since he was known to have made an attempt at it only a year ago. That somebody was yourself, George Elwin.'

Appleby paused for a moment—not, it might have been perceived, for the sake of effect, but in the interest of achieving concentrated statement.

'So you, George Elwin, arranged the body of your brother Arnold, and arranged the weapon you had used, in such a way as to suggest something fairly close to a repetition of that known attempt at suicide. You strapped your own watch to the dead man's wrist. The clothes in the house would hang loosely on him—but he would be found naked, sun-bathing in a fashion you were known to go in for—and who would ever be likely to notice the discrepancy with clothes tidily laid away in their wardrobes and drawers?

'The dead body, maimed in the face as it was, would pass unquestioned as *yours*: as George Elwin's, the owner of this

house, that is to say. And that's all! You had abruptly lost
your true identity. And, ceasing to be George, you had lost
what is probably a substantial fortune. But at least you had
an identity to fall back on—that of your brother Arnold,
whom you had killed—and you weren't going to be charged
and convicted of murder.'

'But it's not *true*!' The lanky man seemed to be in blind
panic. 'You've framed me. It's a plot. I can prove—'

'Ah,' Appleby said, 'there's the point! If you are, in fact,
George pretending to be an Arnold who is really dead, you'll
have a very stiff fight to sustain the impersonation. But if, as
you claim, you are really Arnold, that's a different matter.
Have you a dentist?'

'Of course I have a dentist—in Montreal. I wander about
the world a good deal, but I always go back to the same
dentist. At one time or another he's done something to nearly
every tooth in my head.'

'I'm uncommonly glad to hear it.' Appleby glanced at the
Chief Constable. 'I don't think,' he murmured, 'that we
ought to detain Mr Arnold Elwin further. I hope he will
forget a little of what has been—well, shall we say, conjectured?' He turned back to Elwin himself. 'I'm sure,' he
said blandly, 'you will forgive our exploring the matter in
the interests of truth. You arrived, you know, when we had
not quite sorted out all the clues. Will you please accept our
sympathy on the tragic suicide of your brother George?'

'You mean to say,' the Chief Constable asked half an hour
later, 'that I was right in the first place? That there was no
mystery?'

'There was none whatever. George Elwin's gloom was
deepened by the visit of his useless brother, and he killed
himself. That's the whole story.'

'But dash it all—'

'Mind you, up to the moment of your charging that
fellow with murder, I was entirely with you. And then I

suddenly remembered something that didn't fit—that £5,000 you found here in an unlocked drawer. If George had killed Arnold and was planning to *become* Arnold—or anybody else—he'd certainly have taken that money. So why didn't he take it?'

'I can see the force of that. But surely—'

'And then there was something else—something I ought to have seen the significance of at once. The dexamphetamine in the medicine cupboard. It's a highly efficient appetite depressant, used for dieting and losing weight. George Elwin was slimming. On this occasion, I imagine, he'd come down here principally to do so. It was the latest expression of his hypochondria.

'He could lose fourteen pounds in a fortnight, you know—which would be quite enough to require his taking up one hole in the strap of his watch. And in a month he could lose thirty pounds—which would very decidedly produce your effect of the giant's robe on the dwarfish thief. George Elwin's first call, had he ever left here, would have been on his tailor—to get his suits taken in.'

The Chief Constable was silent for a moment.

'I say!' he said. 'We did give that unfortunate chap rather a bad fifteen minutes.'

Appleby nodded soberly.

'Perfectly true,' he said. 'But let us be thankful that one of Her Majesty's judges isn't burdened with the job of giving somebody a bad fifteen years.'

COLD BLOOD

'THE PELLOWS,' APPLEBY said, 'are all eccentric. Charles Pellow was a case in point. He was just beginning to make a name for himself on the stage when he threw up the career for no reason at all and took to meddling in archaeology. Then he did some exploring. And after that he bought himself a hotel.'

'Pots of money,' I said.

'Well, there was certainly money in the family. Charles's father, Adrian Pellow, was a very wealthy man indeed, and it was understood that Charles was his heir. I don't doubt that the old gentleman had put up the money for this rather grand pub. Father and son were certainly on quite good terms, and Adrian would come down from time to time, quartering himself in a self-contained flat in one wing. That was the position when I happened to go down there myself for a couple of weeks' sea fishing.'

'It was a seaside hotel, with that sort of thing laid on if you wanted it?'

'Yes—a pleasant enough place on an unfrequented and rather rocky stretch of the South Coast. I enjoyed my fortnight's holiday very much. But it had an unexpected ending.'

'Connected with the eccentricity of the Pellows?' I asked.

'Most decidedly.'

'Adrian Pellow,' Appleby went on, 'was a picturesque old chap with a flowing white beard. He didn't very often emerge from his own quarters. When he did, it was mostly to go for solitary walks along the coast, poking about among the rock-pools. He wasn't exactly unsociable, but at the same time he had an odd impulse to keep his distance. It seems he believed the country to be on the verge of anarchy, and full of thugs, toughs, muggers, and violent criminals generally. He was liable to wave his stick in a threatening way if any perfectly harmless stranger showed signs of approaching him. Even with his acquaintances he would quite often converse at shouting distance.'

'Wasn't that rather tiresome?'

'Yes, it was. And the old gentleman had violent political convictions. Every now and then he would stride through the lounge, or appear at a window or on a terrace, and bellow a sentence or two directed against the Government. Behaviour of this sort must have been a little awkward for his son Charles, who naturally didn't want his guests embarrassed. After a few days, as a matter of fact, it struck me that some of them were getting edgy. And I concluded that it had struck Charles that way too. He seemed to be taking the *hotêlier's* first and almost instinctive precaution in such circumstances.'

'Rather more to eat?'

'Just that. Or rather, in this case, a great deal more to eat. Our meals became quite astonishingly lavish. It was almost puzzling.'

'Perhaps,' I suggested, 'Charles Pellow was thinking of throwing in his hand as a hotel-keeper, just as he had as an actor and an archaeologist? Perhaps he was doing you all, as it were, a final blow-out?'

Appleby shook his head.

'It would have been a colourable theory,' he said. 'But in point of fact, it turned out to be much more a matter of funeral baked meats. At least, they might almost have been called that, although it would have been just a shade premature. For it was about a week after this that old Adrian Pellow was found drowned. His body was washed up among the rocks.'

*   *   *

'An accident?' I asked.

'So we were at once assured. But it quickly got round our isolated little community, somehow, that Adrian had probably committed suicide. The fact that his conduct was on the dotty side naturally encouraged the idea. I accepted it myself, even before a small piece of definite evidence turned up. I had a notion that the act was a product of Adrian's having convinced himself that the country was even more on the brink of ruin than usual. His mind had become so obsessed with that sort of imagination of disaster that it had entirely lost its grip of sober reality.'

'One hears of that sort of thing,' I said. 'Of course there is always some underlying mental disturbance. The anxiety about the state of the country and so forth is a mere rationalisation.'

'No doubt.' Appleby didn't seem much impressed by this. 'But as to its being suicide—well, as I've said, something like evidence did turn up. A note was found on the body. It was no more than a couple of lines on the top of a sheet of writing paper. Their immersion in the sea had made them almost indecipherable. But they could, in fact, just be made out. What Adrian Pellow had written was: "*I have taken this step at the earliest possible moment.*" What would you make of that?'

'Some final vision of national catastrophe had come to the old chap, and he had wasted no time in getting clear of it.'

'Actually, we were soon obliged to admit that the reference was to something altogether more rational. It emerged at the inquest that Adrian Pellow had made an extensive settlement of his property some years before. That meant, of course, that he had to survive to a certain date if his trust deed were to be valid.'

'And it was?'

'Indeed, yes—but only just. His death appeared to have taken place just a couple of days after that date had passed.'

*   *   *

I thought for a moment, and then glanced mistrustfully at Appleby.

'It *sounds* plain sailing,' I said. 'Adrian Pellow stuck it out until he knew that his son Charles would benefit by the settlement becoming valid in law. And then he drowned himself with a clear conscience.'

'You've forgotten something.' Appleby was smiling happily. 'You've forgotten what had been happening to our hotel meals that week.'

I stared at my friend. He appeared to be talking nonsense. But that, of course, wasn't his habit.

'Explain yourself,' I said.

'Very well. Those heavy meals gave me one or two sleepless nights. In more senses than one, they may be said a little to have upset me. Particularly in the light of one perplexing piece of medical evidence, which I'll mention in a moment. However, in the end I did tumble to the truth. It was no more than a matter of suspicion, however, until Charles Pellow broke down under questioning.'

I was horrified.

'Charles Pellow! The wretched man had murdered his father? What you were confronting was parricide?'

'Nothing like that. He had found his father's body in a rock-pool. Adrian Pellow's death was indeed a pure accident. But it had happened a fatal week too soon. The settlement was invalid. So Charles, you see, had a problem. He also had a deep freeze. All progressive hotel-keepers have.'

'My dear Appleby!'

'Yes, it isn't pretty. In fact, a cold-blooded affair.' My friend seemed unnecessarily pleased with this disagreeable joke. 'And so I am reminded about that crucial piece of medical evidence. Spine-chilling, in a way. When first examined by the police surgeon, old Adrian Pellow's corpse had been a good deal colder than a corpse should be. Ever!'

'How extremely—'

'So you see what had happened. Charles had turned everything out of that deep freeze, and deposited his father's body in it. Then he told his staff—they were bewildered young Spaniards, for the most part—some plausible story about the mechanism having broken down. That was why we had those tremendous meals. The ordinary refrigerator wouldn't hold all that food, and it would have looked decidedly odd if Charles had suddenly consigned it all to the incinerator or the pigs. So it had to be eaten. And hotel guests are never very reluctant to turn pigs themselves. Little else to do, you know. So—as I said—funeral baked meats.'

'But surely Adrian Pellow would have been missed?'

'Remember that he did for himself in that self-contained flat. And remember that Charles Pellow was a professional actor. He simply impersonated his father—briefly but effectively, every now and then. Adrian's extraordinary habits and mannerisms made it easy.'

I was rather dazed by this time.

'And then?' I asked.

'When the right date came round, Charles got out the body and—so to speak—drowned it again. Full fathom five thy father lies. When found, the quite late Adrian Pellow presented every appearance of an almost freshly drowned man. Restaurants, after all, play very much the same trick with trout.'

'My dear Appleby, trout can't drown.' I was rather irritated by Appleby. Policemen ought not to be flippant, to my mind. 'But what about that note? The one about the earliest possible moment, or whatever the phrase was.'

'Adrian Pellow used to put in a lot of time writing indignant letters about this and that to the Prime Minister and the Archbishop of Canterbury and I don't know whom else. He just had enough sense not to waste stamps posting them. Charles did a rummage through the pile, and came on this particular fragment. It seemed to fit neatly into the picture, so he planted it on the body.'

'Wasn't that a piece of rather muddled thinking? A man about to drown himself would *leave* a farewell note behind him—not take it to sea with him. Anyway, it merely emphasised—'

'I quite agree with you. But Charles Pellow was actually committing one crime, remember, and I expect he was irrationally afraid of being suspected of committing another. That fragment of his father's writing made the death seem explicitly a suicide. And of course it supported the appearance of its not having taken place too early.'

'But the wily Charles,' I said, 'was caught out in the end.'

'He was, indeed. As your banker will tell you, my dear fellow, it's dangerous to rely on frozen assets in a crisis.'

THE COY MISTRESS

'CAB, SIR?'

Appleby and his wife turned round in surprise. One does not expect, emerging from a small *albergo* on the Simplon Pass, to be greeted—and in theatrical Cockney—with just that.

But it was undoubtedly a London taxicab. Two young men had just been settling themselves down in it. But now they had jumped to the ground, and were grinning cheerfully and hospitably at the Applebys. They were—it seemed they couldn't be other than—English undergraduates. Nobody else tours the Continent in that sort of conveyance. The cab, Appleby noticed, had its name—The Coy Mistress —painted on the bonnet.

'Let us take you as far as the hospice, sir,' said the first young man. 'There's another hundred metres after that. So you can still say you've walked across the Alps.'

The young men, in fact, were in such high spirits that it seemed a pity to turn one's back on them. Which was why the Appleby's drove up to the Simplon Hospice in a London cab.

The following day The Coy Mistress turned up triumphantly in the streets of Lausanne. Appleby hailed it—rather regretting that he didn't have a well-rolled umbrella with which to make this metropolitan gesture—and invited its owners to lunch. It was an entirely agreeable occasion. One of the young men, whose name was Ronald McKechnie, recited Byron. You could sense that he adored that supreme poet of adolescence, but he managed a great air of finding the heady verses absurd. The other youth, Peter Lawson, had been told that the site of Edward Gibbon's villa was now occupied by a post office, and in this prosaic circumstance saw a striking instance of the degeneracy of the times. Appleby felt very old, but found all this entertaining, nevertheless. And then the young men returned to the endlessly satisfactory topic of The Coy Mistress.

'You see,' McKechnie said instructively to Appleby, 'a taxi like that is a tremendously good buy. I don't know if you know anything about the London police?'

Appleby, whose job was running the London police, replied soberly that they were a body of men about whom he learnt a little more from time to time.

'Well, they're terribly good—or perhaps it's the G.L.C., for I'm not sure—about seeing that taxis and so on are kept in sound mechanical order. So you can't buy an old taxi that hasn't been inspected and passed in that way some time within the preceding twelve months. But what makes it *really* good value is if you know about Stubbs.'

'And everybody doesn't,' Lawson added quickly. 'In fact, sir, you mustn't tell.'

'He's a little man in Camberwell. For some reason he's not allowed to buy as many of them as he wants—or not direct from the taxi people. So he's open to buying a few back every year from people like us who have been round the Continent in them. Stubbs has promised to take The Coy Mistress off our hands as soon as we're done with it, and he's giving us £25 more than we paid for the thing in the first place. So you see how one should keep it quiet, and only tell one's friends.'

Appleby nodded—by way of honourable assurance that he would not hasten himself to Camberwell on his return home.

'Quite so,' he said. 'But what does this excellent Stubbs do with the cabs when he's got them?'

Lawson chuckled happily.

'He exports them to Ubangi-Shari. At least I think it's Ubangi-Shari, but it may be Chad. Not, you might say, as going concerns. The engines are taken out, and they're converted into carriages for the higher nobility. Drawn by dromedaries.'

McKechnie looked at his watch.

'I say! Peter and I must be going. We're shoving The Coy Mistress into a garage for the afternoon. To a fellow who knows just how to tune up that sort of engine. We'll be going across France like the wind.'

'Or like dromedaries,' Appleby said. 'By the way, was it Stubbs who told you about this tuner up of London taxi-cabs in Lausanne?'

'Yes—that was Stubbs. He's a tremendously smart chap.'

'He sounds just that to me,' Appleby said.

The Applebys flew home.

'You really do quite fatally attract crime.' Judith remarked. 'We go off for a rather quiet sort of holiday, and a chance encounter runs you straight into a spot of smuggling . . . You say it is smuggling?'

'Oh, yes—it's certainly smuggling. How tiresome that I'm pretty well obliged to do something about it. A policeman's lot is not—'

'Yes, I know. But at least I hope, John, that the young men won't get into trouble. They're bound to feel awful asses, poor dears.'

'The young seldom feel asses for long.'

'And they'll be down by £25—the money they were going to get from the benevolent Stubbs. What would Stubbs's line be, do you think? Watches?'

'Almost certainly, as the racket starts in Switzerland. And the whole picture may be called excessively clear. A set-up like The Coy Mistress represents about the last word in obtrusive innocence. Young men like that would never have either the means or the inclination to smuggle anything more than a fountain pen or a bottle of brandy. Customs people are going to treat them very cursorily.'

'But the man who they thought was simply going to tune up their engine has really stuffed the upholstery and so on with thousands of watches for the benefit of this improbable Stubbs when The Coy Mistress is made over to him?'

'That is indeed the picture—and "clear" is barely the word for it. "Pellucid" would be my own choice.'

'Yes, John, I suppose it's extremely simple. But don't forget to tell me how it ends, all the same.'

'Pellucid but untrue.' Appleby had just got home from Scotland Yard one evening a week later. 'It was all too art-less to be authentic, don't you think? Anyway, our young friends are now in gaol, along with several other people.'

Judith looked at her husband in dismay.

'Ronald McKechnie and Peter Lawson? Our under-graduates?'

'To begin with, they're not undergraduates, and never have been. We were dim-witted to be taken in. Consider the business of their giving us that lift up the Simplon. It wasn't, somehow, quite in character. If we'd met first and had a bit of talk, then the sort of young men they appeared to be might have made the offer. But that sudden "Cab, sir?" business didn't ring true.'

'That sounds like wisdom after the event. And I don't see how—'

'Nor were you right in speaking of our *chance* encounter with them. It was planned. In fact, they planned both en-counters—the one on the Pass, and the one in Lausanne. If I hadn't asked them to lunch, they'd have run into us again and asked us to coffee. And then out they'd have come with all that stuff about Stubbs.' Appleby smiled. 'Stuff even a policeman couldn't fail to get suspicious about.'

'I still don't see what they hoped to gain by it all.'

'A magnificent diversion. They knew I'd have The Coy

Mistress traced, and that when they landed it from the car-ferry the whole resources of the customs-house would be turned on to ransacking it. That would mean only a very light and routine check on other vehicles on the same ferry.'

'And it was on one of those other vehicles that the big load of uncustomed watches was really being smuggled?'

'Yes, of course. By the time that The Coy Mistress was found to be perplexingly innocent after all, the whole trick would have been successfully accomplished. But once I tumbled to what was the real plan, every car was of course searched thoroughly, and the whole piece of trickery defeated. In fact, The Coy Mistress should have been called The Decoy Mistress. That's not a very good joke. Unworthy, really, of what was rather an ingenious conspiracy.'

THE THIRTEENTH PRIEST HOLE

'A ND DO THE Poynts still live here?' I asked Appleby, as we stood together with a little crowd of potential sight-seers on the steps of Poynt Hall.

'Yes, they do. It's part of the attraction of the place—that it's still more or less lived in by the original family. Although what Richard Poynt in fact has done is to carve a small modern flat out of one wing. To try and use the whole house would be pretty comfortless, I imagine. It dates from a time when you put on your warmest clothes to go indoors.'

'You know this present owner?'

'Barely. We are more or less neighbours, as you can see. But I've done no more than pass the time of day with him, and I don't think he'll recognise me. Richard Poynt is a retiring sort of fellow, and goes about very little. His earlier life is said to have been marked by some obscure misfortune —"tragedy", as people say—from which he has never really recovered.'

I was surprised.

'But didn't you say,' I asked, 'that we'll see him as part of our money's worth now?'

'It's quite probable. He often takes a party round himself. I've noticed that a number of people who show their houses seem to think it the courteous thing to do. And Poynt has quite a turn for showmanship. Particularly in the matter of the priest's holes.'

'Ah, yes.' I pricked up my ears. For I had been told about these unusual attractions of Poynt Hall.

The Poynts were a Roman Catholic family, and Poynt

Hall was chiefly famous because one of Richard Poynt's ancestors had expended fabulous ingenuity in constructing hiding-places for the priests who, at the risk of their lives, had gone secretly about the country in the time of the Penal Laws.

'I think you said there are twelve?' I asked.

Appleby nodded.

'Yes, you'll see twelve. And there's a thirteenth that is never shown.'

'Because thirteen is an unlucky number?'

'Not exactly. If Richard Poynt takes us round, he'll explain. He makes quite a little drama out of it.'

And it was in fact the owner who showed us over Poynt Hall. He was in late middle-age—grey-haired, tall, and distinguished. He collected our entrance-money without a shadow of awkwardness, and then at once began a pleasantly informal but clearly well-practiced outline of the place's history. His sentences dropped from him easily and with little pauses that gave a great effect of leisure. He might simply have been our host, responding to our interest in his house, but careful not to obtrude upon us more information than was desired.

There were almost a dozen of us—sightseers of the slightly specialised sort that makes its way to the remoter and smaller show places of England. But only one of our number, an elderly American who appeared to be by himself, showed much sign of any relevant knowledge, whether architectural or historical. He was following Richard Poynt's remarks closely, and more than once I found myself glancing at him with curiosity. I had the impression that there was something obscurely familiar about his cast of features.

We were half-way up a shallow wooden staircase when Poynt stopped and tugged at one of the treads.

'And here,' he said, 'is the first of the places you have perhaps particularly come to see.'

*　　*　　*

It was certainly an extremely clever hiding place—a small square chamber concealed beneath a sort of trap-door constituted by two of the steps. The American pressed forward and regarded it curiously.

'I guess this one would have been the first to be constructed?' he asked.

'We believe that to be so.' Poynt seemed slightly surprised, and then went on with his explanations. It struck me now that beneath his courtesy there lay a deep reserve; that here was, in fact, a singularly proud and sensitive nature. Appleby, I concluded, had shown tact in not claiming Poynt's acquaintance upon this faintly commercial occasion.

The tour continued. Poynt Hall, although impressive for its antiquity and mellow beauty, was not really a large place, and it was possible to linger pleasantly in its comparatively few principal chambers. Its compactness rendered all the more remarkable the sequence of hiding places which were revealed to us.

And they were a great success with the little crowd of sightseers. As a panel slid back, a solid bookcase turned on a pivot, a fireplace revealed the rungs of an iron ladder, there were gasps of admiration and surprise. It was like stuff out of a boy's adventure story. I thought how strange it was that Richard Poynt's ancestor should have combined with the grim and honourable business of protecting the priests who came to him this sheer virtuosity and exuberance in adding priest's hole to priest's hole.

The American went on asking intelligent questions and even offering relevant information. He seemed to make Richard Poynt a shade restless—and at the same time to be himself a little nettled by Poynt's particular blend of courtesy and reserve. But he was, at the same time, quite as much a man of breeding as our *cicerone* was. I felt it to be a curious confrontation.

Presently the twelfth priest's hole—a very small one in the floor of a privy—had been revealed to us.

'And that is all,' Richard Poynt said, 'so far as those strange hide-outs are concerned. There is in fact a thirteenth such refuge. But it is never disclosed. An interesting family tradition—at least, interesting to me, ladies and gentlemen—attaches to it. When religious tolerance had been established, and those of us who belonged to the older faith no longer needed such places for the protection of their priests and chaplains, the head of my family decided that one should nevertheless remain secret, and with its whereabouts known only to one Poynt in each generation. I am permitted to tell you that it is a small square chamber with just room for a chair in which a man can sit. But the tradition forbids me to show it to you.'

'I can't say I ever heard of this before,' the American said.

'Possibly not, sir.' Poynt was displeased. 'But so, never-theless, it is. The idea was, of course, that one cannot tell what revolutions history may bring about. The time might always come when an inviolate hiding place would again be useful. The thought was not wholly an idle one.' Poynt paused, having spoken with some warmth of feeling. And the American at once asked another question.

'And when, sir, do you figure it that this tradition began?'

'It dates from the end of the seventeenth century.'

'Now, I find that a surprising thing. For it smacks more of the beginning of the nineteenth century to me—when folks got around to reading Sir Walter Scott's novels. Most ancient family traditions in England date from about then, I guess.'

Poynt made no reply to this mild gibe—which, as I happened to know, historians of literary taste would have had to accept as fair enough. The two men had now defin-itely got across each other. Our party moved on into a bedroom, handsomely equipped with Tudor furniture,

Against one wall was an unusually large *prie-dieu*, elaborately carved.

'That's very fine,' the American said, and stepped over to it. Poynt watched him, and gave a curt nod.

'Yes,' Poynt said, rather drily. 'It has often been admired.'

And now something wholly surprising happened. The American studied the *prie-dieu*, frowning slightly. Then he put out both hands, and gave a quick twist to a pillar. The whole massive object—complete with a handsome breviary or missal displayed on it—moved sideways. We were looking into a small square chamber with a single chair. And slumped in the chair was a human skeleton.

There was a moment's silence—and then somebody screamed. I glanced at Poynt, who had gone deathly pale. Then Appleby stepped forward, grasped the *prie-dieu*, and swung it into place again.

'That,' he said firmly to the company at large, 'is simply rather a macabre joke which Mr Poynt prepares for over-curious visitors. We move on.'

Later, Appleby explained. He had had a brief talk with the owner of Poynt Hall.

'Our American friend,' he said, 'is a Poynt. Once you are informed of that, you see the family likeness at once. His branch of the family left England centuries ago, but he takes a keen interest in his English connections. He knows all about the architecture of the Hall and its various priest's holes. And, of course, he was quite right about the thirteenth hole. The tradition about keeping it secret is a comparatively recent affair. But it proved very useful to Richard Poynt when, years ago, his younger brother Edwin, a ship's officer, who was thought to be dead, came home in some deep disgrace, and then died in the night.'

I was astounded.

'You mean—?' I began.

'Just that. It was something about a sinking ship. Edwin

simply ought not to have survived. But now, by an extraordinary chance, he had died of some injury he had received, and before anybody except his brother Richard knew of his arrival. So Richard simply put the body where he was quite sure it couldn't be discovered. So Edwin had *not* unworthily survived his disaster—or so it could be maintained—and the family honour was saved.'

'But afterwards?'

'Richard could simply never bear to go back to the thirteenth priest's hole.'

For a moment I considered this extraordinary revelation in some bewilderment.

'And now,' I said, 'nothing much need be done?'

'Well, I suppose poor Edwin's bones must now be laid more decently to rest.'

'And that's all?'

'That's all.'

'Appleby,' I said after a moment's silence, 'would you say that, as a policeman, you have acted in a wholly regular way in this matter?'

But Appleby didn't seem impressed by this question.

'My dear fellow,' he said, 'it's obvious that one must back up a neighbour. Incidentally, however, this shocking affair has a moral. However commodious one's cupboards, it's wise to clear out the family skeletons from time to time.'